MADDIE SHIRKOFF
WORLD OF ODDS

Danit Knishinsky

Opuntia Press
Opuntia Press is a division of Opuntia Payments LLC

Copyright © 2021 by Danit Knishinsky
DanitBooks.com

Library of Congress Cataloging-in-Publication Data
Knishinsky, Danit, 2007–
Maddie Shirkoff: World of Odds / Danit Knishinsky

ISBN 978-0-578-87551-4

Printed and bound in the United States

SCAN ME

Dedicated To…

*My father, Ran, my mother, Alma,
my sister, Yael, and my dogs, Capser & Chloe*

To Doobi…

*You were the most caring and
kind dog a girl could wish for*

CONTENTS

CHAPTER 1
DISCOVERING THE PORTAL

Maddie stared at her notebook. Not enough. She scribbled down a few more words. Perfect. One three-thousand-word essay completed! It was such a relief to be done. Maddie Shirkoff had been working on this essay for days but couldn't seem to find a decent topic. "How can you change the world?" her teacher had asked, earlier that week. Maddie could think of many things that could change the world. No more pollution. No more littering. No more bullying.

But Maddie's ultimate answer was: THE PEOPLE. Most things that have been problems in the world were because of the people. Of course, some problems were natural causes, yet Maddie was beyond proud of herself for thinking of this answer.

After all, there was no better way to finish the day than with an essay fully completed and an appointment on the books to head to the world's greatest sport!

"Maddie!" called Maddie's mother. "Come here this instant! You are going to be late for figure skating!"

Maddie hurriedly grabbed her bag and stuffed her notebook inside it. She had lost track of the time and would be arriving incredibly late if she didn't move quickly. Maddie gave one last look at her bedroom before slamming the door shut behind her.

"Coming, Mom!" Maddie yelled back. She pushed herself down the stairs before taking a quick stop behind her mother, who was on a business call. Maddie's mother didn't seem to notice the young girl behind her. Maddie crept silently to the back door of the house in order to avoid one of her mother's favorite things to do: tardiness lectures.

Maddie passed by a mirror that was located in the hallway. She remembered when her six-year-old sister, Avery, would step up to this mirror and insist on looking at herself ALL THE TIME. Maddie gave herself a good stare. She tried to notice all the features about herself that she wouldn't have usually paid attention to.

Maddie had dark brown hair and chocolate brown eyes. Her hair was the color of burnt umber with highlights of coffee brown. She was your typical eleven-year-old girl who had a passion for just about everything.

Her skin was slightly tanned, and she was told that she looked and acted like her mother in many ways. She was very fit, and she knew how to take care of herself.

Maddie was very athletic and was an ice skater. Sometimes she wondered why she always chose to practice full time sports.

She loved to engage in sports since she had the privilege to ice skate every day (but not when it went down like this, and she was late yet again!). She was constantly being yelled at for being late. Now, she might just make it to practice without being told that she had officially been the latest person to ever step foot at the ice rink.

Maddie absolutely adored figure skating. Living in Arizona, it was the best way to abandon the heat. Maddie took off through the back door of her house as she sported a brand-new club jacket with the words Maddie Shirkoff on the front. To her, the name Maddie Shirkoff was the best name she could ask for.

But you may be wondering…why would the name Maddie Shirkoff mean anything to this young girl? The name didn't mean much to others, but to Maddie, it was like a symbol of power. She loved that her family was involved in the development of one of the most famous amusement parks ever; she came from a long line of family members who attended ivy league schools, and they KNEW how to play sports. Any sport. You name it.

Maddie was in a great mood today because she had just celebrated her eleventh birthday and had beaten the snobby brat Charlotte during a jump contest at the rink. This contest was between her and Charlotte, and Maddie's victory had only made her day even better. She recalled arriving to explain Charlotte the rules.

"Now… you start over there. I'll go first. We will start with something easy. Axel," Maddie said in a calm voice. An axel was one of the most basic jumps for a skater who has been doing the sport for a while. It was hard, yes, but if you had your doubles, the jump was incredibly simple. One and one-half turns. Not hard at all.

"Ok," Charlotte sneered, "easy for me! I don't know about you, loser." Then she laughed a high-pitched, cold cackle.

"Save the laughs," Maddie growled, "because who knows. You might fail miserably."

"So, you're saying I will fall super hard and lose this competition?" she glared at Maddie, a smile etched across her face as if she already knew she would win.

"No. I'm just saying don't be so sure that you will win. You never know," Maddie concluded briskly.

A crowd had formed around the two girls. People eagerly waited to see which one would run away in tears. But the crowd knew. These two girls were some of the best skaters at the rink. And if someone crossed them, they were bound to find some sort of problem arise. The difference between Maddie and Charlotte, however, was that only Charlotte got incredibly mad at situations. Maddie was a patient person.

Even though people were mean to Maddie, she would only fight back if the situation was truly horrible. Maddie and Charlotte had been throat-to-throat ever since they could remember. Maddie moved to Arizona when she was only six. She had been to many different rinks, but only the rink she was at now really impressed her. All the skaters were very friendly, and they always made Maddie feel welcome (except for Charlotte, of course).

Maddie advised the crowd to take one giant step back. Charlotte claimed the challenge would be the easiest thing she had ever attempted. They had performed their usual warm ups, Maddie working harder than ever before. Stroking around the rink, stretching before hard spins, and doing the basic jumps to get started.

She had to prove to Charlotte that she was capable of being a better skater, friend, and just a better person in general. Each of them landed their axels up to double flips perfectly. Maddie couldn't help but replay the perfect double lutz she performed, and the cheated double lutz Charlotte had barely accomplished during the middle of the competition ("I didn't get a proper warm up!" Charlotte had whined).

It was these tiny moments like this, which quickly make Maddie's day. She hated mean people, so by showing a mean person who deserved to be treated nicely, she pleased herself and others. These "others" included her friends and family. Maddie remembered when Charlotte angrily threw her jacket on the floor and stormed into the locker room, only to realize that she had entered the boys' hockey lockers.

Maddie had laughed incredibly hard that day. Other things, such as mean teachers like her 2nd grade teacher, Mrs. Mardova, made Maddie want to bang her head against the wall multiple times and have her mother put on a beastly mom look accompanied by a good two hour talk with the principle about Maddie's confusing, complicated, yet incredibly funny life. Maddie's mother had a business personality. A meeting was due if something was wrong. However, if the meeting did not go as planned, Maddie's mother than would lose her calm demeanor and would storm out of the room, making this idea just as bad as all the other ideas Maddie had come up with involving her mother and school.

Maddie was quite fond of taking hikes, so it was no wonder that when Maddie ran out the door wearing her favorite hiking sneakers, dirt trailed everywhere. Her mom DEFINITELY wouldn't be happy when she got back. Today, it was Maddie's turn to watch their dog, Sparky, her brown furred bundle of joy. That little dog had been with Maddie for the entire day, including being her companion on the hike. That meant, both of them were leaving mud tracks wherever they went. Normally, the mud tracks would lead to the rink, but when Maddie saw a glowing white light emanating from somewhere in her quiet neighborhood, that's where she headed. She reached the ball of light in about 5 minutes since it wasn't far from her house.

When she finally arrived in front of the ball of light, she stared intently at it. It was a swirling ball of white light around twice the size of Maddie. Maddie was about four feet, eight inches for her age so seeing something this tall was quite the view. Staring at this giant ball of light made Maddie shiver. Could it really be more than a ball of light?

Maddie's FIRST instinct was to go back home to find her mother. This could be dangerous, after all. But, a part of Maddie insisted she walk through it and discover it for herself. Almost like a fairy tale. Plus, what would she say to her mother? *Oh yeah, 1 more thing. I was walking to the rink and saw a ball of white light. I want to jump into it. Do you mind?*

Maddie's mother was quite a nice person. She did everything she could for Maddie. Maddie's father was at work all day, leaving Maddie's mother with the children. Maddie has 1 sister named Avery who is only six. With her mother being the only person watching the kids all day, especially one who was in the first grade, Maddie had learned to rely on herself. So, one can't blame Maddie for getting distracted without anyone by her side to say, "DON'T GO INTO THE RANDOM BALL OF LIGHT!"

She was willing to step into the ball of light but just for a quick peak. Her parents would never have allowed her to enter the light, however. But what if there was something adventurous that waited for her on the other side of that step? She stared at the giant ball of light. She felt like she was hallucinating. What are the odds of a ball of light from a fairy tale just sitting in the middle of a boring, quiet neighborhood? Well, the best way to know was to jump in. She hopped in with Sparky and in a flash, they were gone.

CHAPTER 2
THE LAND

Maddie tumbled onto her bottom after falling down a very steep hill, which seemed to be a mile long and incredibly painful. She stood up, groaning, rubbing her back that took an unfortunate hit from her fall. As she checked her surroundings, she realized that the ball of light must have actually been a portal. The giant and terrifying portal had transported her to a different world. She didn't know where to. Checking to see Sparky was by her side, he barked when they met eyes. Good, she thought. My dark brown bundle of joy is still with me. Then she began to look around intently at the landscape.

The land looked pretty normal. Trees with blooming flowers shone brightly against the sun. The grass seemed to be incredibly lush and well taken care of.

The sky was a lovely blue and the clouds appeared to be cumulus clouds. They were fluffy and looked like giant pieces of cotton candy. Odd silhouettes seemed to rush by Maddie. But, when she turned around, she saw nothing. The only idea that terrified her about this world was whatever inhabited it. She had read books and had fallen in love with the fantasy genre. But seeing creatures from those books and myths in real life made her nervous.

To the right of her, was a unicorn horn that seemed to be laying on the ground, the large and tall pieces of grass slowly covering it from view. It was clearly no longer on the unicorn, as if it was cut off. It just lay there untouched. Where was the unicorn? She didn't know. But just knowing that it could belong to a unicorn terrified her. Or the bugs flying around? They seemed to change form. Fly. Wasp. Bee.

No skating. No Mom. No Dad. No Avery. No things she knew about. This world was beyond what she had ever had to experience. She realized, sometimes, when you are trapped in a bubble of comfort, you don't tend to really notice what exists around you. And you DEFINITELY don't bother thinking about killer fly-wasp-bees...

As she looked up to check out the sky, the sun's glare hit her harshly. Staring closer upward, she recognized the glare to reflect off something shiny. Almost like a scale? Suddenly, a group of big, red spheres came flying towards her.

She screamed, as she stared at the huge red spheres.

It was a group of fire breathing dragons! There seemed to be nine rows, five dragons in each row, all huddled around one large dragon. The center dragon was crowned with jewels and held a deathly stare. Its eyes seemed to say: If you cross me, you are dead meat.

"Everyone for themselves!" Maddie cried as she ducked behind a rock.

As the dragons landed, their sparkly, red, and shiny scales shone throughout the land. The odd-looking animals surrounded Maddie, who cowered down onto the ground, trying not to be noticed. One of the dragons in the front was quite smaller than the others. They had clearly seen Maddie because they walked straight in the direction of the polka-dotted rock where behind, Maddie hid herself. Of course, a polka dotted rock was the least weird thing she had seen here!

She had begun to panic. When the dragons approached close enough, she could make out bits of what the dragons were saying. "The thing has quite an unusual look," said one.

"It is so ugly!" another one scoffed. Maddie couldn't help but roll her eyes. Just at that moment, the smallest dragon that she had just seen peaked over the rock. Its color was a bright apple red. And its scales were as shiny as the sun. Its eyes looked innocent and curious. However, the innocence in its eyes didn't stop Maddie from freaking out. She began to sweat and unleashed quite a few words that even left a few of the dragons baffled.

She scanned her surroundings, looking for a body of water to hide under it or at least a couple of big trees to hide behind. Maddie took off running in a random direction. Her clueless dog, Sparky, happily trotted along. He clearly doesn't know we're probably about to become dragon food, she grumbled to herself.

She ran, stopping to catch her breath for a few seconds before realizing those could possibly be the last big breaths she might ever take. She looked at Sparky, annoyed that he wasn't also panicking. She took a right and bumped into a tree. The tree opened its eyes and said, "Oh! You big old klutz! Can't you see I'm living here?! I can't move so it would be kind of you to WATCH OUT!" he yelled quite loudly.

"You can talk?" Maddie asked in a whisper.

"Why, of course I can talk! What am I doing right now?!" he screamed. This entire experience so far had reminded Maddie of a children's story book. Something random that popped up every few seconds. She was one for adventure, but adventure in an orderly manner. She liked everything that way. Of course, she sometimes bent those rules, but the point is…nothing here seemed to be in order at all!

All of a sudden, a deep voice began to speak. Maddie looked up and noticed it was another tree speaking. The tree was incredibly tall. A good seven feet. The tree had dark circles in its bark, which were meant to stand in as eyes. They looked tired, as if experience ran through what the tree would call its head. The bark on the tree looked a lot like wrinkles. If there was such a thing as a wise looking tree, this would be it. Maddie fought back a smile. It reminded her of what her grandfather looked like back at home. Home. The word hit her harder than ever. She had only been in this world for a few minutes and already missed home. No mom. No dad. No Avery.

"Now what did we say about being kind?" the wise looking tree asked the younger (and clearly grumpier and more dramatic) tree. Maddie could not hear the other tree's reply because of a giant roar behind her. While she was talking to the trees (Yeah, I know. You don't hear that every day), the dragons had caught up with her. The smallest dragon looked up. It was looking at an older female dragon who was most likely the small dragon's mother. The young dragon couldn't inflict as much damage as the adults. The big ones, those are the ones who she had to be afraid of.

The center dragon with the crown stomped up to Maddie and grabbed her entire body, including Sparky, with his paw. The dragon was humongous. Imagine a three-bedroom house. Now imagine that house coming to life and being slightly smaller than this dragon. It was HUGE. HUGE. HUGE. Even with Sparky's growling and biting, she knew they had no way out.

Maddie looked helplessly at the ground and watched as all the dragons joined together. They were chanting. It sounded as if they were doing a ritual to please the alpha. To Maddie, this sounded like a bunch of mumbo jumbo.

The dragons brought a stick of fire, something to probably burn Maddie and Sparky. The dragons wanted to eat them. Then she realized in an instant. The chance of her ever escaping from this dragon's hand was an astonishing zero. She didn't know the first thing about the creatures here, let alone this entire strange world.

Maddie watched this all unfold horribly in front of her. She desperately tried to follow, but there was no point. She knew that there would be no way out.

Maddie needed to come to terms that the end was near. But at that very moment, the deepest and loudest roar swept through the land. The dragon dropped Maddie and Sparky out of his paw, causing the two to take a nice BIG fall (not a very pleasant one, might I add). He proceeded to whisper to himself, "No. We have to leave. It's coming." The dragons flapped away, leaving Maddie and Sparky alone and terrified.

CHAPTER 3
THE MONSTER

Maddie looked at the creature. It was drooling from hunger and anger. Its teeth were so pointy that they could've been knives for giants. Why? Because the creature was gigantic. Its color was so dark black that anyone could have mistaken it as the first sign of night. The creature was so tall, it loomed over the land as if this world was nothing more than a miniaturized doll house. It made the dragons look like little ants.

It seemed to be at LEAST twenty feet tall and was plenty terrifying. It had about one-hundred sharp and pointy teeth that would have easily pierced through Maddie as if she was as soft as a scoop of ice cream. Sparky took one look at the horrific monster and took off running towards it.

"NOOOOOOOO!" Maddie cried. But it was too late. The creature had noticed Maddie and Sparky. It would be a matter of a moment until Sparky reached the monster.

Maddie realized that the best option was to chase after Sparky since she couldn't return home without her brown bundle of joy. There would definitely be tons of questions as to why she returned empty handed, if she ever returned.

And when her sister would find out, there would be non-stop screaming and crying for the rest of her life (that is until they chose to buy a new pet). When their goldfish died, (and it was a beautiful goldfish with strikingly gold colors), her sister didn't stop crying until they had purchased Sparky. Her mother had been in a foul mood for two weeks straight. Maddie knew her mother would NOT want to discover that Sparky was gone, let alone deal with any time of crying and screaming from Avery.

Maddie was already scared to death. Knowing her little dog was about to get eaten by a giant monster that she had never heard of before (not to mention in this new and strange land) was too much of a harsh thought to bear. She felt as though the emotions growing inside her would make her combust. She felt scared and lonely. As she watched Sparky run, she felt a burst of anger toward the monster. *NO.* She thought. *Its gonna have to go through me.*

Maddie ran, unaware of her surroundings. "Sparky!" she yelled. She had to draw that puppy's attention.

Apparently, the dog was smarter than he looked. Sparky ran straight for the monster and as he ran, he aimed for its legs. *That can't be possible*, Maddie thought as she watched Sparky go. She figured he was going in for the bite. A bold move, for sure, but not enough to release them from this situation. She knew what she had to do to support his efforts. She ran, just a little bit more to the monster's legs, catching up to Sparky. That's when she realized, the dog wasn't going to bite the monster. He was aiming for the ditch.

The two of them ran towards the ditch and as they went to jump inside, the monster's large hand came crashing down in an attempt to grab one of them. Sparky leaped in hope to protect his beloved owner. This caused the giant hand to miss Maddie and head for Sparky instead. Sparky, not wanting to be the monster's food of the day, sprang up and bit the monster, leaving a one-inch gash through his raging hand.

Turned out the monster didn't like people (much less small sized animals with sharp canines) biting through his hand. The monster grabbed Sparky with his unbitten hand and squeezed intensely. Maddie attempted to save Sparky by rushing up to the monster. But, before she could land a punch, slap, bite, or anything that might suitably annoy a monster of this size, he, with a great swipe of his hand, threw Maddie straight at a rock, leaving her knocked out cold and bleeding. Sparky whined as he felt himself getting crushed, no hope left.

After a few minutes, Maddie regained consciousness. She felt dizzy and nauseous. But after seeing what the monster was doing to Sparky, she regained her energy to fight. The adrenaline pulsed in her veins. She grabbed a sharp rock and ran towards the monster. Sparky barked, distracting the monster from Maddie.

Maddie took advantage of the confusion and ran towards the monster's legs. She stabbed him hard behind his ankle. The monster yelled in pain and dropped Sparky. Maddie was relieved to see her dog breathing normally but was horrified at what she saw next. Sparky was on the ground whining in pain. He was bleeding and all curled up. He had many cuts on his face, along with multiple bruises. A purplish goo emitted itself from all the cuts and bites. It seemed to be turning black around them.

"Come on, Sparks," Maddie said through tears. "I know someone who will help you, and that some-one will be me."

Maddie stared at the monster, who had passed out from pain. "I have a feeling that we are going to face harder problems than what we have just dealt with," Maddie said, looking at the ditch. She scooped up the inconsolable puppy into her arms. The poor thing was shivering and shaking uncon-trollably. To see her dog act in this manner made her feel like she was a bad owner and couldn't keep her pup from getting hurt. She cradled the puppy who was sitting in her arms. Maddie kissed Sparky on his snout and headed with him straight towards the ditch and didn't look back.

CHAPTER 4
THE GOBLINS

The ditch led straight to an underground cave. Maddie was absolutely shocked at how she could not have noticed a large gaping hole in the ditch. The cave was covered in goo, one that reminded her of the slime she made back at home with Avery. The lack of light made the walls appear almost black, and the squeaks of the giant bats made her want to turn around and dash out through the nearest exit. Maddie could hear eerie sounds like the dripping of water or weird splashing noises and howls. Was she nervous? Yes. But that didn't stop her.

She felt terrible for Sparky so she continued to hold him tightly and sobbed the entire time. And it didn't help that Sparky was in pain too. Poor Maddie needed a break. She collapsed tiredly. Sparky, acknowledging Maddie's exhaustion, stopped whining for a moment to let her rest. But, just as that moment came and went, a growl rose from outside.

It was the monster. A mean and cold voice filled the cave. It was so loud that Maddie jumped up.

"Great! Look what those idiots did! Now, that stupid beast will wait here until it's dinner time! I say we make peace with that beast by feeding those idiotic things to it!"

"Samara! Calm down! There is no need to get angry." Just then, a light shone enough for Maddie to see who was talking: Three scaly green creatures that had walked out of the dark. Maddie stifled a scream. The creatures were very gooey and seemed very scaly, almost like a frog. Their long, pointy nails were yellow and brown, as if never cleaned, and their sharp, pointy ears were sticking up, listening intently to the world around them.

They were so ugly that every time they spoke any person would gladly look away. The green goo was also dripping off their fingers. There was one female and two male things. The female seemed to have dirty blond strands of hair streaming down from her balding head. She walked with slightly more grace and posture than the other two. One of the males had two hoop earrings pierced onto his pointy ears, and the other one wore a beaten and tattered work shirt. What were they exactly? Maddie didn't need to know. Because whatever they were, they were too scary. After a second, the strange creatures turned towards her. Their faces were dripping with goo as well. "Santa's elves!" Maddie shrieked.

"Um, no! We aren't Santa's elves! Every Enchanted Elf lives further North. How dare you mix me with their lousy kind?! Next time you offend us like that, you'll be missing a few fingers, girl," said the similar female voice.

"Now, now, Samara, don't get too angry. It's so tiny!" Another one said. It was the voice of a male.

"It?!" Maddie asked, seemingly offended.

The male spoke up once again, "By the way, we're goblins. You should've seen it in the pointy ears and green skin but sure. My name is Brido. This is my sister, Samara and brother, Ragon." Maddie was still really nervous but did not want to show any signs of disrespect. After all, Samara didn't seem so happy with her.

"Please help us!" Maddie begged. Maddie gestured to the whining and bleeding Sparky who was still curled up in her arms.

"That's bad! He might not survive! Here, dogs are heroes! Have you ever heard of the Great Doobi? The best hero ever! Born a hero and died a hero," Brido said dreamily.

"Well, what happened to him?" Maddie asked, now intrigued.

"Well, Doobi won every battle he fought. Not even kidding. Even the last one was a winner. But a tragedy struck. Shortly after he won, Doobi died of heart cancer. Oh, he died a hero all right. He united all four kingdoms of *Enchanted*," Brido said as he wiped a happy tear off his face.

"He also ended up being given a giant palace in honor of his memory. His palace is huge! Doobi was free all right! If you can find the correct magic, you can call his spirit. He can help. Sadly, the area is watched over by an enchantress. And you need a specific potion to be able to see Doobi's spirit," Ragon continued.

"So that's what this place is called? *Enchanted*?" they nodded. Maddie continued, "Seems like a kind of iconic and stereotypical name for a fairy tale world," Maddie stated, staring at the goblin.

"Fairy tale?" Samara asked, looking offended, however, she continued speaking, "*Enchanted* is a place where what your people call the SUPER-NATURAL," Samara added as she took a seat. She seemed much calmer now. "Or what you said: fairy tale characters. I take you to know what Doobi's legacy was if you are so fond of these stories?"

"Was it to be a warrior? Not to show too many signs of weakness?" Maddie asked.

"Tell me you are JOKING," Samara sputtered angrily. Maddie sighed. Doobi was so heroic and important, and she couldn't even figure out his legacy.

"It's fine," Maddie began, "I'm new here," she added a glare at the end to show she meant business. But, Samara dismissed it, showing she didn't care.

"That's alright," Brido said. "But, for your information, his legacy was peace and harmony. If you and that dog received the training, you and your dog might almost be as great as Doobi," Brido said happily.

A small voice filled the room, "I'm Ragon. Well, if you want to save Sparky you—" Maddie interrupted before Ragon could finish.

"You know his name?!" Maddie screeched.

"Are you aware that your dog has a collar," Ragon sighed, "anyway, as I was saying, if you want to save Sparky, you're going to need magic. The cuts are way too deep to heal. Plus, whatever attacked him was deadly. I can see poison marks. That's not good. Depending on what attacked, only certain kinds of magic can heal it," Ragon said. Something about the goblin told Maddie that he was typically good with animals.

"He is really good with animals," Samara confirmed, reading Maddie's mind.

"Ok. If you are so good with animals, tell me what that monster was. The giant one. The one that tried to eat me alive."

"You are gonna have to be just a little more specific than that. There are plenty of monsters here that would happily eat you alive. Many more," Samara started; eyes filled with a hunger to inform Maddie.

"What do you mean more?!" Maddie yelled. When she had seen whatever THAT was, she had been certain there had only been 1 of them.

"There are tens of thousands of monsters like that in this world so it would be helpful to give an accurate description. 'It was big, black, and teethy' is an example of something that definitely won't make the cut," Samara responded.

"Um, ok," Maddie stared at the hard face Samara put on, "It was about twenty, maybe even twenty-one feet tall. The color was a black that looked like the night sky, but all his darker parts seemed to be an oil black. His teeth were humongous. They were completely white except for the dried blood from his prey. His eyes," Maddie paused for a second, for she was looking for the right words to describe the chilling eyes that had pierced her soul like a dagger when he had stared into her. She picked up again, "glowing red...like a-" she had not gotten the chance to finish for she had been interrupted by Ragon.

"Darkness Fangs," he said knowledgeably. "They secrete a poison from their fangs and claws. It slowly kills the creature it touches."

"You couldn't have let me answer?!" Samara said, pouting.

"He's the smart one," Brido said, grinning an ugly and toothy grin.

"Like genius smart?" asked Maddie.

"Oh yeah! Way smart!" Brido said, once again.

"Ahem," Ragon began again, "Darkness Fangs. They have dangerous poison on their nails, so when they attack and scratch, the prey gets injected with a deadly poison which we don't really know how to heal without a very powerful magic. Even I don't know where to find it."

"What? I mean, I know you are a genius and all now, but that made no sense," Maddie said, her face scrunched up in concentration.

"That is as simple as the information becomes," Ragon sighed.

"How many more of these Darkness Fangs are there?" Maddie asked, shuddering at the possibility of more of them.

"Tens of thousands in Enchanted. But millions and millions around the world."

"No way. How are you guys alive?! Those things are dangerous!"

"Out of everything you can run into here, those are the equivalent of a puppy dog," Samara added, glancing at Sparky.

"Yeah! Ever heard of Soul Suckers?" Brido asked with a mischievous grin. The group turned towards Brido.

"Remind me why you started talking?" Samara asked, annoyed.

"You guys were making me feel left out. That's why," Brido said grumpily.

"Um...hello? I need to know what Soul Suckers are." Maddie tried to get everyone's attention.

"Take a guess, bozo. SOUL SUCKERS. THEY SUCK YOUR SOUL!" Samara shouted.

"Everyone, if I may," Ragon began, "We should get back on track."

"Yes! Thank you! I will do anything to try and save Sparky. Please help me!" Maddie pleaded.

"Here's the deal. The only way we'll help you is if you help us. We need you to find us the magic to speak to the spirit of Doobi. Doobi can give us tips to become better and more powerful goblins. We can't live in this cold cave much longer," Brido said.

"Why do you need me? I know nothing about this world," Maddie asked, playing with her hands.

"Simple. We could use a fourth person on the trip," Ragon answered, "you never know what you are capable of. Also, you could help us in the villages."

"Why would we be going to the villages?" Maddie asked.

"Getting supplies. It is the best way for us to get blankets, food, and any other necessities," Brido said, glowing with excitement.

"Well, as nice as you are, I don't know how much I can trust you. You don't understand. I just got here, what more can I get out of a trip to Doobi? And I still don't see why you can't get supplies on your own," said Maddie, wondering how she could pose as any help.

"This is your best chance to save your dog," said Brido.

"As of right now, we're all you've got. You can always go...and spend the night next to that monster," Samara said, glaring at Maddie.

"What do you say? Help us?" Ragon asked.

"Well... all right. But only if you help me save Sparky," Maddie confirmed.

"Deal!" all three goblins said at once.

Maddie knew it would be time to soon leave for the trip. Even with all the help, Maddie felt uncomfortable because she wasn't sure if the goblins were either lying or telling the truth. She would have to carry Sparky all the way as well, which would make the quest so much harder.

"Here's the deal," Maddie said, "we save Sparky first and you go later. Okay?"

"Ummm.... nope." Samara stood up from where she was sitting on the cold, hard, and dusty floor.

"What do you mean, no? This dog is about to die!"

"If he dies on the way to finish OUR quest, then we will pay for his funeral," Brido said in a matter-of-fact tone.

"Look, you guys seem nice enough, but I'm not going to stand here and watch my dog die," Maddie said angrily.

"She does have a point…" Ragon began.

"Not a good one," Samara huffed, "you need to have a bigger reason."

"Well, what if I am a good omen?"

"Bah!" Samara grumped, "how could you and your scrawny dog be a good omen?!"

"Mind you. He is NOT scrawny…I walk him a lot," Maddie began with her nose turned, "you have been trying to get out of this place for a while…have you not?" Maddie pointed out. The goblins mumbled in agreement. "And maybe I am just what you need to get out of this dump," she said, trying to sound more convincing than she felt. She HAD to convince the goblins she needed Sparky's quest done first.

"Well, I guess we could give you a shot...and if we follow you first...we could get a better life?" Samara asked, calmly.

"Promise," Maddie held up her pinky.

"Yeahhh...I don't do that," Samara said, looking at Maddie's pinky like it was something that came out of her nose. Maddie put her pinky down, blushing furiously. After a lot of persuading, Maddie won the argument! It was all worth it!

"And Maddie?" said Brido.

"What?" she asked.

"I recommend you watch out for Medusa or you are TOAST!" Brido chuckled at his own joke.

"Medusa?! Nobody told me about Medusa! Are you serious?!" Maddie screamed.

"So serious indeed!" Brido was still half laughing. After all Maddie had been through, this is what she needed to also be afraid of?! Maddie only wanted to lie down and take a nap.

"Maddie, you get some rest. In the morning, we go," Ragon whispered. Maddie was going to need to get used to their ability to read her mind-or figure out how to keep them out of it! Even though it had been the afternoon back at home, it seemed to be night here! Maddie was exhausted and heavily influenced by her surroundings.

Before Maddie realized it, she had fallen into a deep sleep. In her sleep she had an unusual dream. She was back with the dragons and a harmed Sparky was being eaten.

"Nooo!" Maddie woke up with a start.

"It's time to go Maddie," Samara said as she towered over her. "Let's go find us some magic and save that scrawny dog."

CHAPTER 5
THE PALACE

So, what if this quest to find magic and save Sparky might be very, very, very hard? At home, Maddie was tired of not being praised when doing something great. If she did accomplish to save her dog and contact Doobi, she could be a hero in this strange world. People would say, "Great job!" whenever she passed by. Or they would high-five her wherever she went.

At home, it was always about "Avery this... or Avery that..." Maddie was ready for a change. Just because Avery was younger, she received all the recognition for everything. Avery would draw an ugly princess and be praised beyond measure. Maddie could save a baby from a burning building and simply get a nod from her mother. It was enough to drive anyone mad.

Maddie rose and waited for breakfast. She had slept peacefully regardless of laying on a few moldy blankets on the floor.

"Ewwwww, what is that?" she asked as she sat down on a rock that was supposed to be a chair.

"Goblin Gloop! It's quite delicious you know," Samara said. Maddie took a tiny bite out of the weird, oatmeal looking soup. It tasted oddly crunchy and certainly didn't have a nice taste. Almost like the key ingredients were something that were bound to make anyone gag.

"It kind of looks like slime!" Maddie put her hand out to touch it.

"Our key ingredient is bugs," said Ragon.

"Well, that is disgusting," Maddie added while making a sick face. She proceeded to gasp, "I ate a bit of that!"

"Hey! People all over your world eat bugs!" Samara said, "I read about it in a book, you know."

"Well yeah, but…I don't eat bugs so it's weird for me."

"And about that little comment…SLIME. I bet in your world it is used a lot."

"Samara, it is, just, not to be eaten…" Maddie

turned back to Ragon, "but this really does look like slime!"

"Then I guess you like it. I bet slime is delicious. If this looks like slime, then I'm sure in your world, slime is simply Goblin Gloop," said Brido.

"Of course not! Slime...you play with it. You don't eat it!" she said, glaring at him.

"But if you all did, I'm sure you would like it," he said, taking a big scoop of the gloop and slurping it up.

"Ewww. No, not at all. It's disgusting," Maddie said with a stink eye.

She peered around the cave. She hadn't gotten a good look at it last night because it was so dark. There was a homemade fireplace in the middle of the wall, facing Maddie's direction. It was made of just bricks seemingly piled on top of one another. And possibly glued on with the leftovers of Goblin Gloop. The brown bricks actually made the fireplace look nice. And the decorative wood on top made it look gorgeous with the light shining upon it. It seemed as if they used the leftover wood and carved a nice little design to put the entire thing together.

A portrait of older goblins was hung right above the fireplace, and the frame was coated in gold. There were two other portraits hung side by side on the fireplace. One on the left, and one on the right. Each also had a coat of gold on their frames. It seemed odd that the goblins would complain so much about where they lived, but then again, having all the luxuries in the world would be no fun if you lived in a cave. The tunnel that led to their cave home was lined with many torches for light. But none of them were lit.

The rocks that the goblins and Maddie sat on had been flattened out to be used as chairs. And, the table was clearly homemade. It seemed to consist of a makeshift wood. Maddie was careful not to lay herself on the table in fear of getting a splinter to the hand. There were some brown wooden, rickety, old cabinets. This seemed to be the place where the goblins stored all their cups and plates. The goblins' beds were simply blankets laid out on the floor (they most definitely did NOT have the same feeling as a real mattresses).

Each goblin had their own blanket/mattress and a blanket to cover themselves up at night.

The pillows were covered in a brown dust, but other than that, they seemed to be in good condition. The goblins made their home sound horrible, but now that Maddie was REALLY looking at it; it wasn't so bad.

Samara had Maddie head to the village shop to get some clothes. Of course, only older-fashioned clothes were carried so Maddie purchased a pair of scissors and a few sewing supplies to create make-shift overalls together with a nice, white T-shirt to wear underneath.

Maddie did learn to sew at school from the odd kid on the playground who used to be one of Maddie's only friends. The little boy had been obsessed with sewing, and Maddie, having nothing else to do, simply played along with it, learning how to sew like a champ.

The village wasn't too far away from the cave, so Maddie had no problem arriving at the stores. However, when she arrived, and after she selected her items for purchase, she realized she had no currency. She did receive her items for free after explaining that she needed to make some clothes for a journey. Maddie, however, felt that the shop owner only gave her the supplies after seeing her current outfit in pity. ("No wonder he gave you free items, I would have been shocked at that outfit too if I didn't know you were from another world!" Samara said, snorting.)

After Maddie changed (she had to hide in an empty tunnel further away from the goblins' home to do this) she headed outside. She sat next to a lovely pond next to a few tiny palm trees. This wasn't too far away from the cave. Maddie sat down and wondered if Sparky was going to make it. After all, he wasn't in the greatest condition.

They first stopped at a goblin restaurant. It had more food options so Maddie could get a proper breakfast ("Can't we stop by a human restaurant? The village had some nice options," she had whined, gagging at the way the food looked and tasted). The goblins had also taken her to purchase a nice little backpack for the journey. It was a boring chestnut brown color that had a dark black zipper attached to the front of the pack. Sparky was starting to wake up, so Maddie began to set him comfortably in her arms. When it was finally time to leave, Maddie took one last look at the cave and wondered if she would ever make it back. She was planning to ask the goblins more about the Great Doobi later if she had the chance.

Brido took Maddie to see a beautiful, black female horse with a gold carriage behind her. This was where Samara and Ragon were waiting. "Wow," Maddie gushed. "This is amazing! Why are you showing me this?" she asked, eyes shining with excitement.

"We are going to use this for the journey!" Samara responded, with a happy squeal.

"But how did you receive it?"

"Well...while you were sleeping this morning, Brido stopped by to rent a carriage. In this world, horses and carriages are our main source of transportation. We use them for everything. We don't really have a horse, but the wealthy would have many for each person! Sadly, we can only use it up to the royal land. After that, we are on foot," Ragon said.

They all piled into the carriage and Ragon offered to lead. *Where he learned to do this*, Maddie thought, *no idea*. Everyone was quite relaxed that morning. Maddie stared out the window. The birds were chirping, and it was very windy. The ride was incredibly long. Not to mention that it didn't agree with Brido's stomach at all. By the time they had been riding for a solid hour, he looked even greener than when he started.

"I'm gonna be sick," he complained to Samara, who was sitting right next to him.

"Brido, if you vomit on me…SO HELP ME. You won't have anything to vomit with after I am done with you," Samara growled. Brido had stopped complaining for a good while after that.

"So," Maddie began, trying to break the silence, "do you guys have music?"

This seemed to cheer them all up a little. "Oh yes. Samara is obsessed with the band "Goblins 4 Life"! To me, their music is enough to make my ears bleed. I, however, am classier and like the Royal Symphony," Ragon stated. He began to ramble on and on about how classy they were and how beautiful the royal music was that Doobi used to listen to. Thankfully, even the horse became bored, because a few seconds later, his voice was drowned out by the annoyed neighs of the stunning creature.

"So…what about you Brido?" Maddie asked. Brido just shook his head and proceeded to vomit out the carriage window. This was followed by Maddie staring in shock and disgust.

"I'll handle this," Samara began. She slapped Brido twice on the back of the head, the second slap harder than the first. "Now, where were we?" she said as if nothing had happened.

"Hey!" Brido cried. The color had finally gone back to normal on his face, "it is not MY fault I get carriage sick!" he said with a pouty face.

"It doesn't matter if you get carriage sick, but PLEASE! Try your best to keep it in you!" Ragon said, clearly annoyed. Samara slapped Brido over the head with her hand once again.

Maddie was so utterly disgusted that she refused to talk to any of them for the rest of the carriage ride. She spent the remainder of time surveying the land. It looked so gorgeous that she couldn't help but "ooh and ahh" at almost everything ("Would you please stop oohing and ahhhing every time you see something?!" Samara asked, annoyed.). Maddie had vowed not to talk after the vomit incident but eventually, something caught her eye that made her speak.

As Maddie stared, she noticed a tall palace that shone so brightly that it reminded her of dragon scales. The outside of the palace had gold lights surrounding it and the brick was a happy brown color. In the center stood a beautiful garden in the shape of a heart. So many roses and daisies. Maddie felt happy. *But in this world, not a single feeling lasts for long,* she thought.

"Look! We can cross that land and then—" Maddie didn't get the chance to finish because at that very moment, Samara interrupted her.

"Whoa, wait a sec, do you realize that that is the land of the king and queen? We need their permission to cross. It would be so much safer to take the long route. The king and queen's land would take three days at the least," Samara said.

"Ok, then how much time would the longer route take?" asked Maddie.

"About three weeks. It's also much safer," Samara added.

"Are any of you aware that Sparky is dying?! I don't even know if I have thirty minutes left with him!" yelled Maddie who was now on the verge of tears. That's when Maddie realized that the castle was just like the one that her grandfather used to tell her about when she was a little toddler.

He always ended with, "Now Maddie, remember that there is a possibility of another world and for that I give you this key necklace, so you remember to always let your imagination flow through every door," Maddie looked down at the necklace that hung slightly below her neck. It was in the shape of a key. The key was painted in gold and had words on it that said: *A trusted advisor*. Maddie never paid much attention to the necklace but mostly to her grandfather's stories. And this castle was in the story: The Missing Princess. He always talked about how he was never there when the story was told. The fact that it was a story and not real life had always made it funny to young Maddie that he spoke about the tale as if it was based on a real one. A story or tale he missed being there for.

"Fine. If we go in there, to the king and queen's land, I want to search for Doobi artifacts," Samara said so sternly that it brought Maddie out of her memory. Ragon opened the door of the carriage to let everyone out, leaving the carriage in place, separating the horse from it. The horse neighed but was soon taken in by the palace guards who seemed to surround the castle and apparently didn't care that there seemed to be a royal carriage being left out in the sun. The two remaining goblins jumped off the carriage and Maddie followed their lead.

Ragon strayed the path and focused on the large variety of flowers that happened to be in the royal garden. He hopped over for a split second to get into the middle of the perfectly arranged garden before letting out a shout.

"Youch! I tripped over something!" Ragon yelped. As he fell, he grabbed Maddie, who had followed him into the garden, to help him keep his balance, but he only made them both fall. His foot had apparently gotten caught on a piece of metal bearing out of the floor. Ragon looked underneath himself. It was a trapdoor. The trapdoor had words in gold written on it. Maddie squinted to see what the words were but they seemed to be covered in dust.

She brushed the dust aside to read:

> *Advisors only. Our gift to you and your descendants for your deed towards us.*

Maddie pondered over the message but formed no real understanding of it. A keyhole was showing on the trapdoor. Maddie put the words aside and focused on the keyhole.

"Umm. I think this could mean something," Maddie said as she glanced at the keyhole that bore out of the trapdoor. It couldn't be missed. It had to mean something.

"Well, thanks captain obvious, but I think we all figured that out," Samara said, "wait one second, what's that necklace you're wearing?"

"Pfffft! This old thing?" Maddie asked looking down carelessly at the necklace that now had a few ugly scratches from the fall with Ragon.

"Yes. That old thing, give it to me," Samara said hastily. Maddie removed the necklace just in time for Samara to grab it without scratching Maddie hard on the arm. Maddie watched as Samara took the key and placed it in the keyhole. Each goblin crowded around, making it harder for Maddie to see. As Samara opened the trapdoor, a shiny and unmistakably powerful glow shone in their faces. Each goblin gave a look of awe at what was inside the door. Maddie, however, had absolutely no idea what the object was or what was even happening due to her terrible view.

"What is it?" asked Maddie. She was shocked to see the dirty look given to her by Samara.

"You're obviously not ready yet," Samara said, almost inhaling whatever was in there, her face was so close.

"What she means to say is that you will find out at the right time and that time just isn't now," added Ragon. He had spoken so little in the entire journey that Maddie had forgotten he was even there. Maddie had only then realized that each goblin was crucial to the group's success in accomplishing the mission. Here's what Maddie realized:

Samara- She can be strict and keeps the group on track. Loud and outgoing.

Brido- Funny but gets off track and doesn't enjoy having "know it alls" around.

Ragon- Smart and is very quiet. His smarts keep the group from having life issues (having no food, no water, and no money). He is also kind and caring and has a way with animals.

Maddie had absolutely zero idea whether her grandfather had been to this world after the opening of the trapdoor, but she put that thought aside and focused on Sparky. Ragon tenderly wrapped Sparky in a blanket he had packed earlier. Maddie watched as Sparky closed his eyes under the strength of whatever medicine Ragon had just given to him.

It was supposedly a mix of different plants from the royal garden that Ragon secretly grabbed. The problem was, Ragon couldn't guarantee that Sparky would ever wake up. It wasn't what he had given the dog. It was how weak the dog was that made the problem so horrid. Maddie watched as Sparky licked her face as he had done so many times before. Tears rolled down her face uncontrollably. This could be the last time Sparky would ever lick her, so she took in every moment.

"Who are you?" came the voice of one of the guards. It was one of the males. Maddie turned around to see Brido stuffing whatever was under the trapdoor into his bag. Two guards stood side by side. Two puppies.

"The Royalis guards!" Ragon whispered.

"The who?!" Maddie asked, confused.

"Royalis! That is the name of the Royal Family!"

"Royalis? Oh! Ha! I like that! Royalis...kinda like royal. Isn't the name perfect?" Maddie said, grinning stupidly.

"Maddie! Be quiet!" Samara whisper-shouted, "you're talking like an idiot isn't going to help us get past these guards!"

"Ok, Ok," Maddie whispered back, "you don't have to be so mean about it," she pouted.

"Both of you! Enough!" Ragon said, intervening, "The last thing we need is to get into trouble!" he continued, "and I need you both to get along for just a FEW minutes! Just enough time to get us into the castle! Those dogs aren't as innocent as they seem!"

"Oh," Maddie felt her stomach tie itself to knots, "will we get in trouble? Wait...they are kind of cute...aww," Ragon pinched her.

"Don't underestimate those dogs, Maddie..."

There was a sweet looking female who was just a little chunky and short, making her look so innocent and adorable. But something about her told Maddie that she would sometimes have a temper and a vibe that said: *Don't touch me when I'm eating or am tired or when I am sleeping or doing anything unless you are giving me a belly rub. I love you!* Standing next to the female dog, stood a skinny but muscular male puppy who was so very cute and seemed to have a vibe that said: *You can touch me or pick me up, I don't care I just wanna give love.*

"Ha! Like we wouldn't be able to pass you! You're so tiny! But we will still follow your rules," Samara added after seeing the glare that was swiftly given by Ragon. "um, how old are you exactly?"

"15 weeks," the female said proudly.

"But we are getting bigger every day!" piped up the male.

"You two are stunning golden retrievers. Doobi was an amazing Golden Doodle. What are your names?" Ragon asked, awed by their beauty.

"I'm Chloe and this is my brother Casper," the female, Chloe, said.

"Well, let's get going. We need to see the king and queen. I suppose you need help getting up the stairs?" Samara asked mockingly. Samara went to pick up Chloe but as soon as Samara's hand touched Chloe's stomach, Chloe jolted around, teeth bared and attempted to bite Samara's hand. It happened incredibly quickly.

"Don't ever try to pick me up again you stupid goblin!" Chloe snarled, teeth still bearing. Samara got the message and set off to follow Chloe up the golden steps leading to the castle doors. Samara, Brido, Ragon, and Maddie followed, moving much slower than the two puppies in front of them.

Casper gave one last sorry look and set off to catch up to his sister after saying, "Be careful. She'll use the fact of us being Doobi's brother and sister against you," The goblins stood there gaping as they followed the two dogs going up the steps. Each goblin and Maddie were in awe at what they had just found out: These two puppies were related to the Great Doobi.

CHAPTER 6
THE ROYAL FAMILY

The only possibility now scaring Maddie was meeting with the Royal Family. As soon as she stepped into the humongous castle, she could tell they meant business and were not going to tolerate having a complete stranger walk into their land unless they were to be trusted. The king and queen sat on top of their solid gold colored thrones.

The thrones were lined with designs that were meant to fit each personality of the royal. Each royal had a cushion on a seat of a dark red color. Next to the king and queen were smaller thrones that clearly belonged to the children. Only one seat was occupied on the children's side, however. Maddie fidgeted with her hands, nervous to speak to the king and queen. The good and lucky thing was that they seemed to be perfectly normal humans, that was until Maddie needed water.

"Um, excuse me ma'am, I don't want to bother you, but may I please have a cup of water?"

Maddie prepared herself to look at the Queen and was shocked to find a beautiful black-haired woman. She was incredibly fit and skinny for a woman who was always wearing a ballgown. But, then again, wearing the gown alone was a workout itself. She wore an amazing silky ivory and gold threaded ball gown that was very soft and light. It was accentuated with tulle on the skirt and it seemed to put the dress together perfectly. Her tiara was filled with diamonds, left and right. It seemed that the queen hardly noticed the size of the jewels on her head and that she seemed to not feel the weight of the heavy outfit pulling her down.

Having looked at the queen in awe, Maddie decided that the king was equally as handsome. She saw him wearing the royal red color that had strips of gold. His cape was of the same shade red with streaks of gold making a wave pattern. His pants went down to his ankles and he wore gold colored wrist cuffs. The only similar item shared between the king and queen was a ring on their finger made of diamonds. Behind the king and queen was a plaque which read: "I am my beloved and my beloved is mine". The king stood up and said, "My name is King Caimal and this is my lovely wife Queen Rosa—,"

"All hail the queen!" shouted the crowd of servants wondering around. The crowd truly adored their rulers.

The king continued, "My beautiful wife Queen Rosa! And over there," the king said as he gestured to a pretty girl around nine years old. She wore a pink gown with crystals as dots and a tiara like her mother's, "is one of the most important people in my life, Princess Luna." Maddie was now dying of thirst. Luna rose from her throne and held out her hand. Maddie went to shake it but was shocked that the princess pushed her hand away. Instead was a little fog, and a swirl appeared around her palm. Almost instantly, a cup filled with water manifested in the princess's hand. That's when Maddie realized how they were different: this family possessed magic.

"Maddie! Look at your face!" Brido laughed as he made a stupefied look the way Maddie had been gazing at the water. Luna still had been holding the water respectfully, knowing Maddie's shock. Maddie took the water politely and bowed to Luna, which followed by a nice well deserved thank you. Maddie was simply amazed and couldn't have employed more respect with her bow and thank you. The king stood up and retrieved the now empty cup of water from Maddie.

"I can't help but notice that you all seem very tired and most likely need a place to rest tonight," the king said, a mysterious glint in his eyes. He proceeded to sit back down and used magic to make the cup disappear.

Maddie looked at Ragon who seemed very pleased with this idea. Samara on the other hand was eyeing Chloe nervously. But, it seemed all the goblins would be excited to spend the night in the royal palace. The king seemed to understand they wanted to stay because he rose and gestured towards a long hallway filled with paintings of past royal *Enchanted* rulers. As the king led Maddie and the others to the room where they would be sleeping, Maddie heard whimpering. She looked over at Ragon.

She saw him stop, bend over Sparky, and quietly shake his head. That's when it hit her: Sparky was beginning to die. Something had to be done or she would lose Sparky forever. She stared at Ragon. As soon as he noticed her watching, he picked up Sparky and smiled to make it seem as if nothing really happened. But, Maddie knew the truth. And if she didn't ask for help quickly, Sparky might die today.

"Maddie?" Princess Luna inquired. "are you alright?" Maddie was completely oblivious to the tears streaming down her face as she looked at Sparky. Maddie ignored the question and continued to walk. She felt that a night with Sparky in a somewhat normal-like-home area would alleviate her homesickness.

"Right here." Princess Luna gestured to a room on the right side of the hall. It was one of the many rooms located in the hallway. The hallway had been made of beautiful brown bricks. The previous *Enchanted* rulers all had their pictures hung in every hall, making it look like the royals were trying to summon thousands of ghosts at once. Although the hallway and entrance were incredible, Maddie couldn't stop gaping at the room.

It had four beautiful beds. The window had a view of a lake with a fountain. The curtains were white, and the room walls were adorned with a white and gold colored wallpaper. Each bed was a four post, with luxury blankets and pillows to make the night as nice as possible. The bathroom contained a diamond-laden bathtub and sink. Clearly, whoever built this palace possessed high living standards. The bathtub had an incredible view, looking out to the entire city. Which city? Maddie had no idea.

"We're all staying here?!" Maddie said, gaping at the room. Luna simply giggled.

"Your majesty, I thank you for allowing us to stay here," Ragon said with a little bow.

"Yeah, um, thanks," Maddie said awkwardly. She went for a bow and promptly tripped over her shoelace, causing her to take a tiny fall. Luna, unfazed by this, held out her hand in order to help Maddie up.

"Well, it is late. So, I shall leave you to it. Good night, fine guests," Princess Luna said sweetly.

As Maddie lay down on the bed, she looked at the goblins then Sparky and realized that she needed something done right away. And the only helpful solution that popped into her head was to sneak around the castle to see what magical and helpful ingredients might be lurking in corners not meant for others than the Royal Family's eyes. Maddie thought back to the moment she had spoken with the young girl in the village.

She had been walking around, heading to the shop when a little girl around the age of seven came up to her. "What are you wearing?" she asked quizzically.

"What do you mean?" Maddie had asked, offended. To her, at the time, she didn't understand why people didn't seem to appreciate her style. So, a question like this seemed to annoy Maddie a bit more than usual.

"Well, it's not every day a child comes into our village dressed like that!" she said with a suppressed giggle.

"I come from a different land. This clothing in my land is quite popular," Maddie responded, trying her best to sound professional.

"I suppose it could be," the girl began, peering at the outfit with a slight look of distaste, "but here, well, I've never seen anything quite like it."

"Look, I am going to call the spirit of the Great Doobi. My companions are planning to go with me."

"Hmm. And I supposed you want to cross through there?" the girl pointed to the king and queen's land. However, Maddie hadn't known it belonged to the king and queen.

"I guess that would work, yeah."

"Well, do you see that gorgeous palace over there? That's the castle! And I hear they have the most lavish rooms, hallways, and meals. One time, a young boy in my grade told me they have SECRET rooms as well. Hidden with all sorts of magic that would benefit us in many ways. Of course, it is hidden from the public. Nobody would DARE to steal any of it," she said, a mysterious glow casted upon her little face. Maddie had stared, unwillingly drawn toward her stories.

"What is your name?" Maddie asked the girl.

"Kaya. I've lived here my entire life. So, forgive me if I am all over you...we don't get many visitors in this village."

"Oh. Well, thank you, Kaya. I really should be on my way now," Maddie said as she turned around, getting one last look at the little girl.

An abrupt sneeze from Samara jolted Maddie out of her memory. Kaya had told Maddie about the secret magic here. Magic that nobody would dare to steal...if Maddie grabbed it, she might find one strong enough to save Sparky. *What secrets could be unraveled from this family?* she thought, mind racing.

As the stroke of twelve on the clock drew nearer by the minute, Maddie was wide awake. No signs of exhaustion were allowed to show. This entire time Maddie debated whether to steal her way through the castle but, in the end, the argument always ended at: *this is for Sparky.* She knew sneaking around the king and queen's castle to most likely steal bottles of magic seemed like a stupid idea. And, it was definitely not one of her greatest.

At the stroke of midnight, Maddie peered at the other side of the room to make sure the goblins were sleeping nicely in their lavish beds with their thick sheets and tended pillows. Maddie kissed Sparky's head making sure to not wake him up and then she slowly but quietly left the room. She whispered, "This is for you, Sparks." And proceeded to head out the bedroom door.

CHAPTER 7
MIDNIGHT AT THE ROYALIS CASTLE

As Maddie opened the door to exit her room, she felt a scary sensation develop at the pit of her stomach. As if she was doubting all the choices that she was planning to make. She kept walking, hoping that all the emotions building up inside her would go away. That if she stopped the death of her brown bundle of joy that meant so much to her, all her problems would be resolved. Then, she would finally be able to go home. See her mother and father! And as annoying as she was, Avery. But she couldn't do that until she saved Sparky. After all, taking him to a world without magic was like setting him onto his deathbed.

Sadly, Maddie could not guarantee that the magic she was searching for would be strong enough to heal Sparky. His condition continued to worsen. Maddie took another step. The sinking feeling went away because Maddie accepted that whatever consequences might happen, she would face them with a healthy Sparky by her side. Maddie crept through the hallway and decided that she needed to check the king and queen's room. But there had to be a way to distract Casper and Chloe. The only problem was that the queen let it slip that the puppies had training and would be hard to distract.

Maddie realized that there had to be some magic in other areas that would somehow defeat Casper and Chloe. She figured the magical ingredients would sit in the kitchen. After all, it seemed like this would be the natural place for herbal ingredients. She hoped she would find a magic cookbook alongside those many magical ingredients. The family also might have a stash of weapons which Maddie felt would come in handy when defending herself against guards. As Maddie took the first step into the kitchen, she was flabbergasted at its beauty.

Though the curtains covered up the windows, Maddie wondered how gorgeous it could possibly look in the daytime. The huge window offered a perfect view of the *Enchanted* horizon and mountains near the garden. The kitchen had counters made of diamond. An island sat in the middle where a vase stood on top filled with white roses. Maddie realized the castle was entirely white other than the exception of a few rooms. White in this world clearly stood for good.

But if the Royalis castle stood for good, who stood for evil? Maddie tried to get the idea out of her head, but it just seemed to hang there like a lost child seeking guidance from a parent. Maddie arrived at the conclusion that the pantry should have the ingredients that would help Sparky to at least stay alive for enough time for her to say goodbye, spend nice last moments, or find the healing potion that should heal him once and for all. As Maddie searched the pantry, she was shocked and disappointed to find only normal foods.

"No!" she cried, "there has to be some sort of magic in here! Maybe even a trap door or hidden object!" she began tipping cans while trying to make as little noise as possible. She stared at the pantry shelves and remembered one of her favorite ideas from the movies. Maybe some object is actually a passage to a secret door! She furiously kicked and pulled cups and cans off the shelves, but nothing seemed to happen.

The only important idea she could remember from a movie, and it didn't even work. She stared furiously at the pantry. If this family was so magical, where was the secret room Kaya had told her about? What if she was lying? After all, Kaya was seven. She wasn't old enough to be trusted. If Kaya was an adult, then maybe. But Kaya got her information from some little kid on the playground. Why did Maddie ever believe her?

She seemed to be having absolutely no luck with finding anything important until she kicked a cup off the shelf once again, this time in anger. The cup instead pulled forward then ricocheted back into position; it revealed a spiral stairway into a dark chamber lit by torches. *I did it!* As Maddie stepped in, a cold feeling hit her. *It's really happening,* she thought. Now there was no turning back. Maddie knew that it was time to accept that if she didn't walk down the steps, she would lose Sparky forever.

As Maddie slowly made her way down into the chamber, she noticed a lot of mice and bugs crawling around, giving her the hint that this place had not neither been visited nor cleaned in a very long time. It also gave her the idea that this was a place where she could locate a great number of family secrets. Maddie checked her watch and decided to keep walking now that it was 1 a.m. She managed to reach the end of the spiral staircase. There, she stood face-to-face with a giant iron door.

The first thing Maddie noticed about the door was its incredibly large size. It reminded her of the portal except it was much larger. Both this door and the portal had an amazing and magical aura. As if something was hidden behind it. To Maddie's disappointment, she noticed there was a keyhole. The only place the key could be located was the king and queen's bedroom.

Maddie understood this place would be highly guarded but at the same time she understood that she had absolutely no choice. She had come this far and if she was caught now, she would leave empty handed. If she didn't try to find the key, Sparky would die a painful and sad death. His death scared Maddie more than anything. What would she do without the brown furred companion that had been so loyal to her? Maddie quickly turned around, walked back up the stairs, and left the chamber door open while keeping the pantry door shut. She grabbed a knife from the kitchen. Without glancing back, Maddie ran down the hall.

Maddie held the knife tightly in her hand and noticed Casper and Chloe sitting by the door. It was a heavy two-foot knife, almost a sword, really, that would make a loud noise if dropped. Maddie threw the knife in the opposite direction. The two puppies immediately ran in the direction of the sound in order to "catch the intruder". As Maddie snuck into the king and queen's room, she started to feel very nervous all over again. Sooner or later, she would enter a world of trouble. So, she would have to be incredibly careful.

Maddie quietly opened the door to find the king and queen sleeping in a lovely and enormous room. The room consisted of two desks along with a vase filled with red and white roses sitting on a tall glass table. Maddie investigated the room for any sort of suspicious sign that could be related to or pointing towards the location of the key. Maddie decided that she could always search a little more (later tomorrow, of course), but she knew that staying in the castle too long would expose her.

That's when the epiphany hit! The key might be under the queen's pillow. During dinner with the Royal Family, the king stated that he would trust his queen with anything. If he trusted her as much as he said, he would obviously trust her enough with a key that could most certainly unlock the family's secrets!

Maddie crept up to the queen's bed and peered over her. In one way, she felt bad for attempting to steal this key, but the other side of her only cared about the life of Sparky. As Maddie drew in closer to the queen, she noticed that with every step, she moved slower. So much was happening in her life. She needed time to herself, but in this new and strange world, everything around her just kept moving.

Everyone in this land seemed to always have something to do, not allowing her to fully process the fact that she was now alone in a strange and new world with no-one by her side to tell her everything would be ok. She officially made up her mind within that few seconds; she would grab the key, take whatever she needed from the chamber, and use it to defend herself from this crazy place until she found a way home!

Maddie slowly and carefully reached her hand under the Queen's pillow. She pushed her hand just a little more forward and... she felt something! She pulled it out and...it was the key! She decided to take a good look at the object. It was like the one she had worn around her neck. That thought led to the realization that after she opened the door, she would have to retrieve the other key from Samara so she could have a twin set of keys. But just as Maddie was walking out the door, she heard the voices of the puppies.

"That was ridiculous!" Chloe snarled.

"I swear it had to have been one of the guests! I say we check on them right now!" Casper growled.

Maddie only had a limited amount of time to return to her room, then leave again to continue her quest for the castle's magic. She checked her watch and was annoyed to find out that it said it was now two am and she had to "wake up" at six am to continue the journey. Maddie ran down the hall pausing every few seconds to catch her breath. She entered her room and as she quietly jumped back into bed, she clutched the key tighter in order to calm herself down. She held her breath as the voices of Casper and Chloe got closer by the second. As the two puppies came into the room, she stayed extra still in order to not make a peep.

"Hmph," grunted little Chloe angrily. Chloe seemed downright angry at the fact that she now had nothing and seemed to have wasted her time going on a chase for no absolute reason. Maddie heaved a sigh and peered down the hall to see if the two puppies were gone. Maddie quietly rose, ignoring the exhaustion that pulsed through her body. It was like venom, slowly reaching every part of her.

Maddie began walking through the halls to the kitchen. She imagined what would have happened had Casper and Chloe apprehended her. The poor goblins would have also been in trouble...even if they had nothing to do with the situation. Maddie felt guilty in a way because she could only seem to imagine they would receive the worst of the worse punishments. Maddie continued walking until she reached the pantry. Groaning with exhaustion, Maddie pushed the pantry door open. As she walked down the spiral staircase, she found, to her delight, the chamber door untouched and open. As Maddie approached the iron door, she held the key in her shaking hand.

Maddie inserted the key into the keyhole, and she was instantaneously excited to realize that at this very moment, there was a real possibility of returning home. All she wanted was to see everyone she cared about again, to feel the warmth of her mother's touch, and to eat the food that her father kindly brought home every day. She took a deep breath and made sure that she was ready and… she inserted the key.

Maddie watched as the door slid open ever so easily. The door seemed to be old, and because of that, it made many odd creaking sounds. All Maddie could see at first was a dimly lit room with a dark brown desk, a brick fireplace, and a nice crackling fire. As she looked around more, a bookshelf came into view.

5 boxes sat on the shelf. She decided to open each of the boxes and every time she opened one of the dark black boxes with gold decor, she was not too shocked to find spoons and cups to measure ingredients and more tools to help with magical cooking, potion making, and dangerous spells that could

instantly defeat an enemy with 1 flick of the wrist (she made a mental note to try these on Charlotte, the mean girl at the rink, later).

Maddie didn't want to lie to herself. It was one-hundred percent true that she was highly annoyed with the fact that she couldn't seem to find any sort of magical ingredients or a magic cookbook. She knew anything she found would be somewhat valuable but not as valuable as any items in this odd room that were magic. As she was getting ready to leave, from the corner of her eye she noticed a gold door. It was embroidered with diamond designs. Clearly expensive. It was as if it was purchased just for this room, for it fit the wall's and room's designs perfectly. It reminded Maddie of the custom designed items you could simply purchase online.

Maddie tried to open the door, giving it a little nudge. The door seemed to be incredibly heavy, so she tried her best to shove it open. It was clear the king and queen didn't want anyone in here because as soon as she pushed the door open a little bit, a giant ax came swinging out of nowhere!

Maddie ducked with a terrified squeal and backed into the wall. The ax slowly went back to its hidden spot, and the little door that had opened to let it out was once again hidden from sight. Maddie watched with horror as she felt a tiny poke hit her shoe. Nails were coming out of the floor. Bits of clothing and dried blood were on the nails. Clearly, this wasn't the first time someone had attempted to break into the royal magic chamber. Maddie hopped onto a random table, her shoe falling off, left on the floor. Maddie watched as the nails rose, one of them puncturing her shoe. As soon as the nails retreated into the floor, Maddie desperately grabbed her shoe and did her best to place it back on her foot before some other ridiculous trap came to kill her. Nothing seemed to happen next so she went over to the door, finding herself victorious for surviving that encounter.

It had no signs of a keyhole which made Maddie NEED to explore. As she opened the door, she peeked inside, hoping to find magic within the walls of this chamber. To her surprise, every shelf in the room was filled with bottles and bottles of magic. Maddie excitedly began to look around, preparing a bag she snatched from the goblins' cave for the trip. But of all the items Maddie was interested in within the room, only one specifically caught her eye.

A lovely little book laid in the center of the room. As Maddie stepped closer, she looked at the cover and found herself incredibly fascinated at the beauty that was inscribed on the cover page. The design was simple but stunning. The cover was light brown and showed a wave pattern inscribed with gold. As Maddie eagerly flipped through the pages, her smile slowly turned to a frown. It was a book about magical ingredients.

Half of the book contained information about magical ingredients themselves while the other half listed out magical recipes. But, as Maddie searched thoroughly through the recipes, she realized that none would be strong enough to heal Sparky. She had flipped through a few of the healing spells, but each time it ended with the same sentence: magic for minor injuries. But if this was a cookbook with somewhat minor spells for beginner magicians, then what was it doing placed in the center, being the most important feature of this little room? Maddie figured there was a more important book somewhere in the castle. After all, something more powerful wouldn't have been so easy to find. But for now, she had to make her way back to her bedroom.

Maddie crept back up the hallway while she clutched the key in one hand and the cookbook in the other. She seemed to be incredibly weighed down from the amount of magic she had stolen from the chamber. Maddie once again checked the time and was very annoyed to discover it was now 5:30 a.m. *That'll be only thirty minutes of sleep! How will I act natural in the morning if I'm falling asleep at the table?!* Maddie ran as fast as she could to the room, hid all her supplies under the bed, and fell asleep in only a few seconds with Sparky lying beside her.

CHAPTER 8
BUSTED!!!

Maddie wasn't sure if she would be able to rise out of bed that morning only thirty minutes later, but she did anyway. She knew everyone would be too suspicious if she missed breakfast or acted out of exhaustion during the meal. As Maddie trudged down the hall, she searched her bag to make sure nothing had been removed or taken. Luckily, the bag had not been touched, which meant that it was safe to head to breakfast.

While passing through the hall, Maddie watched as the servants solemnly put up a few more pictures of a young girl who apparently belonged to the *Enchanted* Royal Family. At first, Maddie figured it was only Princess Luna. But as she peered closer, it seemed to have been another child about eleven years old. The same age as Maddie. She was wearing a royal blue ball gown and donned a tiara of diamonds like her mother. As she watched the servants put the picture up, she noticed each one curtsying at the picture and lighting a candle. *What could have happened to this child? Who was she?* Questions filled Maddie's head like a swarm of angry bees.

"Ma'am?" Maddie asked a nearby maid.

"Yes, Madam?" the maid responded quite suddenly as if she had been trained to answer inquiries quickly.

"Who is that girl in the picture?" Maddie said, walking up to the portrait. The maid slowly looked at Maddie, as if still deciding and pondering exactly what that answer might be.

"That is Princess Kara," she said, "She was taken from the Royal Family by the evil queen. Kara was playing outside with Casper and Chloe," the maid looked at Maddie then went back to adjusting the picture.

"So that is who the evil is in this world! Queen… um… name?" Maddie asked meekly.

"Lilith. Queen Lilith," the maid shuddered as if it was too terrifying of a thought to allow permission to roam around her brain. Maddie figured that the topic must be hard to talk about for the Royal Family.

"Do you mind telling me a bit about what happened?" Maddie asked thoughtfully.

"I already did. Just not in great detail," she grumped.

"Well, I wouldn't mind if you told me the story in great detail," Maddie shot back.

"I don't like to speak of it. It is a waste of time repeating it over and over and over again. By the time I am done explaining, people like you always have another request or question about the subject. All for that dumb reward the king and queen are giving out to find their daughter. Can anybody just ask about her because they feel bad?!"

"Well, that is what I was trying to do before you yelled at me," Maddie said, annoyed with the maid.

"Very well then."

"Thank you. Now, may I hear the story?"

"Alright. Everyone in *Enchanted* knows about the Royal Family. It is a common goal for many people either inside or outside the kingdom to try and kidnap a member of the family. They could earn great money for doing that. Hold the child and demand money for their return. However, many commoners wouldn't think of harming the children. After all, the royals are like family to them. Although there are guards all around the castle, the children do not need them when they are playing in the courtyard. Kara knew this. Every commoner understands 1 thing. The security outside the castle is protected by magic. No commoner could get into the castle. However, one person could. For one to try and defeat this woman would make them mad. Kara knew she couldn't fight off Lilith. Neither could the guards. They tried very hard to save her, though. But nothing worked. Kara has been missing for a few months now. Three to be exact."

Well that was one heck of a story, Maddie thought. She thanked the maid and continued to walk down the hall. She had to hurry to the breakfast table. She didn't want to look to the others as though she had slept in...that was a bad sign considering her eye-bags were probably GINORMOUS.

As Maddie walked down the hall, she wondered: *Why would the evil queen take Princess Kara?* There had to be a good reason for kidnapping a Royal Family member. As Maddie sat down at the table, she wanted to think of the best way to raise the subject of Kara with the family. If Maddie found the evil queen (and Kara of course), there would be tons of different magical ingredients in the evil queen's lair! And of course, she would be able to save Sparky! Maddie hurriedly ran to the dining hall. Everyone was already seated.

"Dear lord! Maddie looks like she didn't have enough sleep whatsoever!" Ragon said as he peered across the table. As soon as that remark was made, Casper and Chloe looked at Maddie suspiciously. Everyone at the table waited for Maddie's response.

"Ah. Well you see… I was up all night for Sparky. Yes! Sparky! Hehe…" Maddie nervously giggled. The king shot her a confused look. It was as if he suspected something…

"Well. If you were up all night for Sparky, then what was wrong with him, may I ask," the king inquired. But, through the fake smile and tone of voice, something told Maddie that he was waiting for an accidental or jumbled-up response, then he would point to her as the one who stole the key and broke into the chamber. That's when it hit her. She had forgotten to close the chamber door! No wonder the king was suspicious! It was obvious that someone had snuck into the chamber last night! And Maddie was the only one awake at the time!

Maddie scolded herself. *I messed it up!* she thought. *I gave up the fact that it was me by attempting to deny!* Maddie knew that she would have to see how much more she could deny it. But she knew that once the king had found out, she would have to RUN.

Maddie looked at the king and said, "As much as I enjoyed this lovely breakfast, thank you, I understand that my timing for our visit is to be cut short so if I may...would you mind if we traveled through your land?" the king looked boggled for a second due to the quickness of the question. After all, many people would love to spend more than one night, right?

"Sir?" Maddie brought the king out of his thoughts.

"Ah, well Maddie, as you know, the royal land is the safest route. But of course, a challenge always lingers. Therefore, I always need to make sure that the people who are taking this roadway are to be trusted." That word hit Maddie hard due to the fact that she had not been very trustworthy towards the

Royal Family. But her excuse never changed. *It was for Sparky.*

"Guards," the king said, "Check the child's bag." Maddie knew what she had to do.

"No," she screamed! "Get your dirty hands off me!" she cried as one of the guards grabbed her wrist to pull her away from the bag. The goblins were in utter disgust at the fact that their amazing royal stay had been ruined by Maddie's lack of brains. "WELL DON'T JUST STAND THERE! RUN!" she shouted across all the commotion. But each goblin had been handcuffed. Maddie stared in shock.

"I didn't take anything!" she shouted nervously. She hoped she sounded more confident in front of the family than she did to herself. But, Maddie knew. They had figured out what she had done. There was no point in denying it. She would have to fight back. As the goblins stared in disbelief at Maddie, they seemed to understand why she had done what she had done. All of them except for Samara. It was like the two were having a mind war of their own. It went a little something like this...

Maddie: I'm sorry... I didn't think we would get caught.

Samara: Oh, that's ok. I totally understand that you had no clue we would end up handcuffed and grabbed by a bunch of giant, sweaty guards. NO PROBLEM, MADDIE.

Maddie: Really…I had no idea. Why are you so mad? If I knew exactly where the magic was…I WOULDN'T HAVE BEEN UP UNTIL 5:30 A.M LAST NIGHT!

Samara: Good to know. Next time, why don't you consult with us instead of going on to ROB THE ROYAL FAMILY?!

Maddie: It's fine. We will find a way out of this.

Samara: YOU will find a way out of this. Until then, I will come up with ways to KILL you in your sleep!

Maddie: I appreciate your lovely idea, but I am not exactly drawn towards the idea of my death at elleven years old!

Samara: Well, you will end up having it if you don't get us out of this situation!

Maddie: Calm down. I will figure something out. I have an idea.

Samara: Yes. Because I should trust your ideas. LOOK WHAT HAPPENED BECAUSE OF THE LAST ONE!

Maddie: I DIDN'T KNOW!

Samara: THEN YOU SHOULD'VE WAITED UNTIL YOU DID KNOW!

Maddie: And if I did... SPARKY WOULD BE DEAD!

Samara: I DON'T SEE SPARKY DEAD RIGHT NOW! SO, YOU WOULD'VE BEEN ABLE TO WAIT! BECAUSE NOW...

Maddie: Now what?!

Samara: Because now... SPARKY ISN'T DEAD, AND WE ARE HANDCUFFED BY A BUNCH OF GIANT, SWEATY PEOPLE!

The entire argument had gone on rather quickly. But, in the end, they were still handcuffed and said no words except for what was communicated through their looks at one another and angry facial expressions. And neither of them liked the conversation very much. Maddie tried to escape from the guard's grip, but it was no use. They had her locked up nice and tight.

"Take them to the dungeons," King Caimal ordered.

"Yeah! And why don't you murder my dog as well!" Maddie yelled sarcastically. Sparky had been put in a cage.

"If the dog dies, then the dog dies," he said coldly.

"Nobody robs this family without receiving punishment," the queen said.

"But...I was doing it for-" Maddie was cut off.

"SPARKY! WE KNOW!" Samara yelled, "BECAUSE OF YOU, THAT IS WHY WE ARE HERE IN THIS STINKING POSITION!"

"But he-he-he-he's my d-d-d-dog...I want him to be s-s-s-safe," Maddie's body shook and she at once broke into sobs. It was embarrassing to have everyone watch her cry, but they were all so wrapped up in the situation that, truthfully, nobody cared.

The group was escorted down the hall. The guards took an abrupt turn and removed a portrait. Behind the painting was a staircase. The very one that led to the dungeon so many feet below.

CHAPTER 9
TIME TO BREAK FREE!

The guards had managed to stop Brido from whining after giving him a blow to the head. Maddie and the remaining two goblins watched as Brido slumped unconscious.

Samara was outraged. "HOW DARE YOU TOUCH MY BROTHER," she screamed, "I AM THE ONLY ONE WHO IS ALLOWED TO WHACK HIM OVER THE HEAD LIKE THAT!"

"What Samara means is that we will stay quiet until you-" Ragon began.

"I MEAN WHAT I SAID! IF I BREAK FREE OF THESE HANDCUFFS, SO HELP ME!" she shouted, her naturally green face slowly turning a beet red.

The staircase was long. And it was no easy breeze for these guards to carry one incredibly mad goblin, a crying child, and 1 heavy, unconscious goblin. Ragon stayed very neutral. Since each guard took 1 prisoner, Ragon's guard seemed to be incredibly thankful for his choice to grab the quiet one.

The dungeon was gray, with rusted iron, and one single seat for the dungeon guard outside the cell. The group was not pleased to find out they all would share one cell. It was an absolute mess. Samara was happy that the guards had removed the group's handcuffs as soon as they had entered the cell. Luckily, the guard who was on watch duty in the dungeons seemed to be tired, so he fell asleep right away. *Some guard*, Maddie thought. With the entire group in one cell...Maddie had no clue how the guard seemed to sleep so peacefully.

After all, a lot of noise was being made...Maddie sobbing in one corner, Samara cursing angrily in the next. Not to mention Brido's groans of pain. He sat up and asked, "Why did the big, sweaty, hotdog hit meeee? Ooohh...beefy..." then he fell back over once again unconscious. Ragon, however, still had not said a word. Not even with all this commotion.

Finally, he blurted out, "I knew it!"

Maddie looked up, her eyes were red and splotchy, but she didn't care, "What?" she asked, face the same color as her eyes.

"I know how to get out! You guys! Listen up!" Ragon said quietly. Samara and Maddie came to listen. They agreed to fill Brido in once he had woken up.

"So, what do you plan to do? This guy can't be too hard to beat but...the family?" Maddie shuddered to think about it.

"See the guard?" Ragon asked. The two girls nodded, "He's in a deep sleep. He hasn't woken up from any noise. He is already beaten if you think about it."

"Yes...but he's really far away...how would we even get to him?"

"We'll wake him up. He will walk over here, and I will distract him. Once he is over here, you need to grab his keys. I watched him when he transitioned us from the last guards. He isn't very bright. By the time we remove his keys, he will have run upstairs to tell the king. We will have just enough time to break open this cage."

"That will never work!" Samara cried.

"Give it a chance, Samara, otherwise, how else do you plan on leaving this place?"

"It-it's just a dumb plan. The guard is going to be smart, hold us back, and guess the plan right away."

"Samara," Ragon began, "give it a chance. If it doesn't work, do whatever you want to me. But if it does work, well at least just try having some hope. Otherwise, we won't get out of here…"

"Fine," Samara grumped, reluctantly agreeing.

"Alright…then what?" Maddie asked, trying to break the awkward tension that filled the room.

"Then, we grab all the potions and bottles. I noticed that they left them on the dining table. Probably planning to do something with them, so we will have to act fast. Once we have done that, we should be good to go."

Maddie shouted to the lazily sleeping guard, "Excuse me? Excuse me?" no answer, "EXCUSE ME!" she yelled loudly. The guard, startled by the noise, suddenly opened his eyes.

"What is it?" he asked.

"You don't mind coming over here, do you?"

"Well…I'm nah s'posed to. But I guess I could come for a l'ttle…"

"Look at me. And please, don't look at Ragon." Maddie asked, knowing the guard's lack of brain cells.

"Mmk. I won't." *Man, this guy is stupider than he lets on,* Maddie thought with a grunt. Maddie was grateful, however, since he seemed to be the only guard down in the vast dungeons.

When the guard approached the cell, Ragon abruptly grabbed the guard by his shirt collar and snatched the keys around the guard's belt.

"Got 'em!" Ragon practically yelled. Samara shushed him angrily. Ragon snatched the guard's keys from his hands.

"Hey! Y'all took my keys! Can I have 'em back please?" the guard asked. Samara rolled her eyes and laughed coldly.

"In your dreams, buddy. Right now, I have an appointment with FREEDOM!" Samara said happily. The guard ran, just as Ragon had predicted, up the stairs, yelling for the king.

"Ok. Now, we have to open the cage. Maddie, your hands are small enough. Take the key and open the door from the other side," Ragon directed her. Brido began to wake.

"I have a headache…" he moaned.

"I know. For now, follow our lead. We will take care of you once we are out of here."

"Ok," Brido agreed although he didn't know what was happening or what he agreed to. He wasn't too pleased with the situation, but he could hold his pain inside long enough to at least escape the castle. Because at the moment, the Royalis castle was enemy territory. The door swung open. Maddie cried out in delight.

"Run!" Samara cried, "I hear a voice!" there was indeed a voice. Many of them. And they were getting closer every second the group stood there in the same place.

"Run! Follow the plan!" Ragon cried. The group took off running up the narrow staircase, occasionally ramming into one another ("Ouch!" Samara had cried when Maddie had accidentally smacked her in the arm.) They ran into the hallway.

There, stood four beefy guards. Maddie was flexible. She could do a really high, pretty kicks for ballet and skating. In this case, it had to be high, pretty, and painful. Maddie kicked one of the guards in the face, knocking him out cold. Samara punched another guard in the groin. The guard fell to the floor. two down. Two to go. Ragon was going to be attacked from both sides. Left and right. As the guards ran towards him, Ragon stepped back, allowing the guards to run into each other instead.

"We're doing great!" Samara said, high-fiving Maddie.

"Yeah, we are!" Maddie said with a grin. The group ran down the hall and into the dining room. Ragon had been right. Everything Maddie had taken was left on the table. Nobody seemed to be in the room. Maddie scooped up the ingredients and the key (why they had left everything there, unwatched, confused Maddie) and put them in her backpack, which had been left on the chair in which she sat.

"Where is Sparky?" Brido asked. Maddie's face fell.

"The king has him," she replied, on the verge of tears.

"...And you may not ever find him!" a voice bellowed. It belonged to the king.

"Ok. Here is what to do. Samara, Brido, and I will be hiding under the table. The tablecloth is long, so nobody will suspect us. Maddie, you will run and grab Sparky. The king is coming into this room, so nobody is watching the dog. I will throw this croissant I found on the table. It will make a nice distraction. And yes, I could only find this croissant if that is what you are going to ask."

As if on cue, the king walked into the room, and sure enough, behind him, in the kitchen, sat Sparky, in a crate. Ragon threw the croissant, and Maddie took off running towards the other room.

"Hurry!" Ragon whisper-yelled. The king stared at the croissant then looked at the table. Maddie was opening the crate. The king began walking towards the table…Maddie grabbed Sparky! The king began to lift the tablecloth…magic already swirling in his hand…

Maddie quickly hid under the table with the others, clutching Sparky in her arms.

"Why-why would you come back here?!" Samara whisper-yelled to Maddie.

"We can still go through with the plan!" Maddie replied nervously.

"Oh no…" Ragon whimpered, sounding exactly like Sparky. The king shot a ball of magic under the table, almost hitting every member of the group.

Another ball shot right afterwards, under the table, hitting Maddie in the chest.

Maddie tried her best not to make a sound and ignore the pain now forming in her chest. The king began to speak, "I know you are all under there," he said with an evil smile, "but I'll wait...after all, I have all I need," he said, brushing the magic book with his fingers.

Maddie felt the burning in her heart, and she collapsed. Her head would have hit the hard floor if Samara hadn't caught her.

"You guys," Maddie could hear the panic creeping into Samara's tough voice, "something is wrong with Maddie!"

The king stood near the table, chuckling. He knew they were under the table and he didn't seem to care.

"The plan," Maddie managed to say, her breaths becoming shorter.

"Ok. Let's go!" Samara cried. Samara rose out from under the table, swiftly pushing the king back, causing him to topple over. Maddie grabbed the book and the magical ingredients. She tried her best to follow the group. The group ran to the entry doors of the castle where they reached the gates of the king and queen's land. Maddie hoped that the key she had stolen was would be of any benefit. After all, the key may have worked with the door, but that did not mean it would work with anything else. Maddie silently prayed inside her head, hoping the key would work.

"Well don't just stand there!" Samara cried as Maddie fumbled with the key, "put it in already!" Samara snatched the key out of Maddie's hand and shoved it into the gate's keyhole, and it opened!

Maddie felt herself charge through the royal garden, not taking a second to look around her.

"Seize them!" shrieked the voice of a female. Queen Rosa. She had changed. She no longer wore a ball gown but instead, a beautiful outfit that came with leggings and a poofy shirt, one that reminded Maddie of medieval times. To be honest, this whole word reminded Maddie of medieval times. The Queen's hair was done up in a braid, leading down to a ponytail. The beautiful Dutch braid fit her perfectly. But, Maddie did not have time to gawk at her beauty and attire. The queen was not here to receive compliments.

The group hustled, avoiding guards as much as possible. The chase seemed to go on forever. Maddie, being a child with a low attention span, seemed to have forgotten about the chase for a minute, since she stopped by a tree to catch her breath.

"What are you-RUN!" before Ragon could finish his sentence, he turned around and shoved Maddie forward.

"Go," Samara urged them, "and Maddie, don't think I'm done with you!" she growled. The guards were right behind them. The rest of the night had been a blur. There was a lot of shouting and 'Left! Right!'. Maddie had tried her best to run, occasionally giving in to the pain in her chest from the magic, but she never stopped completely.

Maddie felt herself getting dizzy, the world starting to fade to black. She could hear the screams and shouts of the townspeople, and wondered: *what could possibly be going on?* She thought of Kaya, the little girl whose story got her into this mess. Then again, how could she blame Kaya when it was her choice to go looking for the magical ingredients in the first place?

Guards followed the group, weapons ready. Sparky was unaware of what was going on. He simply began to rest his head against Maddie's shoulder.

"No no no no...come on little guy," she said as she stopped to pet his head, "stay conscious for me."

Ragon stopped to look at Sparky, "Give him to me. You are in no condition to hold him," he said sternly.

"I guess that's true," she began, "don't let him doze off."

Ragon gave a nod and picked up the tiny puppy from his owner. Sparky was starting to fall asleep, but Ragon began to move the pup's head in an attempt to keep the dog awake.

They had been chased for a long time but by night fall, the royal guards had given up and returned to the castle. The goblins had set up a nice fire with tree bark they picked up in the area in order to not only protect themselves from monsters by using light, but to also keep themselves warm because in this place, a quick night time chill set in.

"Look guys," Maddie said through shivers and tears, "I had no clue he would find out. I-I just wanted to save Sparky," she cried. The pain in her chest seemed to relax, which was a relief since that meant the spell was just a shock but nothing long term to be concerned about.

"Oh, Maddie. I understand that this dog means so much to you. But you also need to think about the fact that there were others with you. You stole from royalty. And sometimes, you forget, you will be leaving, never having to worry about this world again. But us? We stay. And now what do we do? We wanted a good life, not something like THIS. And...the king and queen were gracious enough to allow us to stay in THEIR castle, and let's be honest, you stole their stuff and destroyed the trust of everyone. I mean, look around," Ragon quietly remarked as he took a sip of warm tea.

This tea had been created with the leaves of the mint plants that surrounded them. Maddie used the bark to prepare a small-sized cup, in which she poured in the lake water. After, she heated it up with the mint leaves she found and *voilà*!

But Maddie was immediately brought back to reality. After all, you can't just remind yourself about making tea and expect everything to be perfect when you come back to the world again.

Maddie turned to see high grass, strange howls, and man-eating plants just a few feet away. She proceeded to look at the tattered green tent in which they were staying in. "Not to be mean but if you hadn't gone around snooping, we would still be in lovely conditions," Samara said, coldly. Maddie looked down at her feet, ashamed of herself. The area around them was scary. If it wasn't for Ragon, one of the man-eating plants would have chewed her up.

Maddie recalled the memory. They had been walking a long time. They found a river and a clustered group of edible plants nearby, so they figured they would set up a camp with what they had. Apparently, Samara had brought blankets at the beginning of the trip. The same thin and dusty ones from the cave. They each set up a blanket on the floor. No pillow. Just a blanket. When Maddie got hungry, she had told the group she was going to search for some food. She found the ingredients to make the tea, and she was about to grab a juicy looking plant when someone yelled, "Don't! Those are *Fang Plants!* You need to be careful around those! They might not be able to move, but if you get to close, THEY WILL EAT YOU UP FASTER THAN YOU CAN SAY 'I HATE PLANTS.' So be careful," Ragon warned, "Just pick the apples out of this tree."

"Isn't it alive?" she had asked, remembering the encounter with the wise and grumpy tree.

"Some, yes. This one technically, no. But yes. As you know trees have cells-"

"Shut up, please," Maddie begged. Maddie was relieved that this tree wouldn't yell at her like the last one. She clearly showed her relief since it made Ragon chuckle.

"Um, Maddie. I just asked you a question. Hello. Can you hear me?" Samara asked, annoyed at the lack of response. Her cold voice brought Maddie out of her memory.

"Sorry. I was just recollecting my thoughts."

"Well, that's nice. I don't really care. Anyway, since we are here, what did you steal from the family? I didn't get the chance to look. We will have to make amends eventually though..."

"Well, I did steal a book of magic and took a few magical ingredients," she said hoarsely. Samara bolted up.

"No way!" Samara went to snatch the bag, but Maddie stopped her, "I thought you only stole ingredients!"

"Wait, I want my necklace back," Maddie said.

"What for?" Samara asked suspiciously. Maddie had stayed up all night examining the key after waking up ten minute after having gone to bed. Turned out, the key she stole from the castle was the twin to her grandfather's key (she had figured this out earlier on). To Maddie, the only useful information in the book was if these two keys were put together using certain ingredients, they would combine to make such a powerful magic that could be used to open an important door. Sadly, the book didn't say which door was part of the legend. Also, it would take all the magic Maddie had stolen.

"Look, it is technically mine and I don't need to always tell you," Maddie said this partially out of anger; this was due to the disrespect doled out by Samara when Maddie only wanted to know what was in the trapdoor. Samara agreed and handed Maddie the necklace that had been in her coat pocket. Maddie handed Samara the book and then crawled to the opposite end of the campsite, where nobody could see what she was doing.

She took out the homemade teacup and started to mix the ingredients together. The recipe required the following:

RECIPE FOR THE TWIN KEY GLUE

- *Syrup from the Maple trees of the Woodland civilization*
- *Salt from the desert of Cacara*
- *Spices from the River Valley civilizations*
- *And a Quartz-Diamond mix from Enchanted*
- *Acid from Lupia*

Maddie had to admit, it was cool hearing the names of other kingdoms in this strange world. After all, these odd and out of place names felt like a whole different area that wasn't even near Enchanted. Maddie couldn't help but think of home, the normal name that made her think, a country, not a kingdom. Maddie dragged her self reluctantly out of her thoughts of home, and proceeded to make her potion.

Although it was her entire supply, Maddie felt that if she had the ingredients…why not? As Maddie poured and blended each ingredient, she became more excited. Once she finished, she couldn't wait to open that door if she found it. Maddie got ready to pour the last ingredient in…acid. None of the ingredients were the normal kind you would think of. They all seemed to be magical versions of it. After they're all melted together, it will immediately be transformed into a super glue tube with the magic glue inside. Maddie poured in the acid and watched in awe as the mixture turned into a tube filled with glue so strong that it could glue an elephant to another elephant and keep it stuck there!

Maddie grabbed the two keys and held them together. They immediately latched onto each other becoming a different shape. The shape formed the head of a dog. But, what could that mean? Maddie was too tired to think anymore so she headed outside and grabbed the book from Samara, while hiding the key in her backpack. Maddie took the cup and placed it in her backpack as well, just in case she needed to prepare another potion. In an instant, Maddie fell asleep. Outside however, the howls of the animals kept the night loud and noisy while the land waited to be explored the next morning.

Chapter 10
Queen Lilith's Palace

Maddie watched as the strange birds made their calls to one another. The glare of the sun hit her eyes with a stunning force that made her want to crawl back into bed and sleep more. After all, when you spend some time in a dark dungeon, and the first form of light you see is the moon...the sun does not greet you very well.

Maddie wanted to believe there was nothing more to do in this odd world. That she would have the ability to go home, see her parents and sister, and hopefully visit some friends. She was quietly thinking of what had just happened when Samara stepped into the homemade tent Maddie had made out of sticks.

"You know, it would be nice if you weren't so

boring and came out to talk every once in a while," Samara grumped.

"Well I'm sorry if I am not coming out because I just spent my first night as a fugitive!" Maddie cried angrily.

"Well I was PLANNING on taking a walk and wanted to invite you," Samara began with a glare, "but then you reminded me we are fugitives because of something YOU did!" she said with a grunt.

"Oh…about that. I already told you I was sorry. Really," Maddie said, tone changing, "I only wanted to save my dog. You don't understand. He's been with me through such hard times," she said, trying her best to keep her hopes up when it came to saving Sparky.

"Well, let's go take a walk with Brido and Ragon. Brido's head stopped swelling," Samara said kindly. Maddie laughed. Samara wasn't so mean ALL the time. Maddie agreed and Samara went out to fetch the other goblins. Maddie rose, tired of wearing the same clothes all the time. The only time she got to change was at the royal palace where she received a lovely new nightgown.

Samara came into the tent, followed by Ragon

and Brido. Ragon looked at her. "Hello and good morning! You ready for that walk?"

"Um, yeah I guess," Maddie said, tone changing to annoyance. She didn't know why she felt that. Almost like she suspected they were hiding something, and she didn't know what. But she felt it was important. Then she remembered. She couldn't understand why the goblins would keep the trapdoor potion from her. It was clear they were incredibly interested in it. Not just because they didn't want her to know what it was.

Maddie took a deep breath and tried her best to calm down. Whatever it was, maybe they had a good reason for it? They were friends. And friends would never do anything to hurt one another. Maddie put on her sneakers and stood up, the goblins waiting for her.

"Come on!" Maddie cried excitedly, "I saw something last night that will blow your mind! I don't know whose it was, but I know you will love it! An abandoned castle!" she cried excitedly.

"An abandoned castle?" Ragon asked, excitement creeping into his voice, "I've never heard of one here! I can't believe it! You found one! Think of all the learning and history and-and-and yes! Let's go! If it's abandoned, we'll be safe. Nobody tends to visit abandoned castles here in *Enchanted*," Ragon finished.

"Why not?" asked Maddie, "back in my world, abandoned castles are tourist destinations. Tons of people go every year!"

"Well in this land, a castle isn't abandoned unless something bad happened within its walls. Deaths or failed treaties or anything that could result in a battle," Ragon explained, looking grim.

"Well, let's go check this one out. For me!" Maddie begged. The group agreed, and they set off towards the abandoned castle. It was not far from the campsite, but Maddie was the only one out of the entire group that noticed it in the first place. The goblins didn't even know an abandoned castle existed over there. Maddie trudged along, occasionally shaking some dead grass off her sneakers.

"How much longer?" Brido moaned, "I still have a headache…"

"It's not that far you, big baby," Maddie said, giggling, "just keep walking. It's only like a forty-minute walk."

"Forty m-m-minute?!" he sputtered, clutching onto his head. "I don't think I will last...I should be with Sparky, sitting in a tent, sleeping!" he complained.

Maddie and the goblins trudged through the grass. "Ragon, you are sure you covered the tent for Sparky to be in there?"

"I'm one-hundred percent sure," he responded, "I also left some food and a blanket for the dog to curl up in. It seems a bit irresponsible of you to just leave him there, however. Especially since it is only sticks. He could find a way to get out. Not to mention his condition or the-"

Maddie glared at Ragon and heaved a sigh, "I know. I trust he will be safe. We will only be gone for a little bit."

The group walked the rest of the way in silence. Maddie saw the castle right in front of her. She gasped excitedly.

"Here it is!" she said, squealing with delight, "Isn't it gorgeous?"

Ragon stood gaping at it. "It's b-b-black...Maddie that stands for evil!" Ragon said, unsure of whether he should take the risk. The castle was a dark black and was rimmed with silver lining on each wall. The grand doors reached about ten feet and were also colored silver. The castle had a very pointed look as well. The top of the castle was basically a needle.

And at the top, was a balcony with a giant hole at the bottom. The hole led down to spikes sticking out from the ground. This reminded Maddie of the secret chamber in the other castle. Whatever was in the moat was definitely not water. The "water" was a dark blood red. It looked as if it was recently added...Maddie shivered but put the thought away, for an abandoned castle should not have guards, and this one didn't.

"This is an evil castle Maddie! I don't want to go inside it!" Brido moaned.

"Calm down! What can hurt you in an abandoned castle? Look! No guards. We'll just go in and check it out a bit, then we can head back to the campsite and deal with your irrational fear of abandoned castles," Maddie said, glaring at him, "This was a surprise for you guys! Just pretend to act excited. Please?"

The goblins reluctantly agreed, and all crossed the giant bridge over the moat of blood. Maddie felt shivers go down her spine but knew as long as it was abandoned, she would be safe. Brido gave a moan and stepped over the bridge, shaking like a scared puppy.

"Can you stop?!" Maddie asked, frustrated with Brido's fear, "I told you it is abandoned! Plus, it USED to be an evil castle, now, with us stepping in as good, it technically doesn't have that evil vibe anymore!" Maddie said, grinning.

"Maddie! When a castle is run by an evil ruler, the castle itself is evil as well. You can't change fate," Samara responded, coldly.

"Ok. Fine. It's evil. Now let's go!" Maddie said, staring at the large silver doors. She began to push them open and found they were locked shut. Then, the doors swung open without any help.

"Ok," she said nervously, "Maybe not evil but it could be haunted..." she whispered, heart pounding against her chest.

"Oh please," Ragon began, "ghosts are good!"

"Yeah! If that's all that is in there, then we're fine," Brido said, "but it's still evil so you never know..."

"We are going in," Maddie said sternly. She was a little nervous. It felt as if the goblins' panic had rubbed off on her. An evil castle filled with ghosts...this wasn't looking like fun anymore...

Maddie took a step into the castle, and a cold feeling washed over her. The main entrance of this abandoned castle had beautiful tiled gray floors. Torches surrounded the hall but none of them seemed to be lit. Then, 1 sight caught Maddie's eye.

There was a gorgeous and dusty table in which dark black roses stood. Even though the castle appeared completely abandoned, the roses that stood on the table were full of life. Almost as if having been watered every day. But a faint glow emitted itself from the roses.

"Maddie," came Brido's terrified squeal, "that-that-that-"

"Maddie, we have to get out of here!" Ragon warned.

"Why? They're just roses," Maddie replied, rolling her eyes. The goblins fear seemed to be rubbing off on her a little bit but other than that, it was just annoying.

"Maddie! There is only 1 way to keep roses in that perfect condition! A preservation spell! IT'S MAGIC! Someone is here, making the castle look abandoned! Maddie, we have to go!" he said.

Suddenly the vase went flying into the wall and shattered into hundreds of pieces.

"Ah, yes," said a cold, cruel voice, "you are the first to find out my plan, but not the first victim," she cackled. Maddie watched as a lady slowly walked up to them. Her dark black hair reached to the middle of her back. Her off-the-shoulder blood red dress was tight to the waist with her sparkly diamond shoes glittering like no other. She had dark brown eyes and a stern face. She had a thin body, and her hair was tied into a half bun half down look.

Maddie stood, gaping, hands closed into fists. "You wanted me to come here!" she yelled, "why?"

"Because I just needed to see you," she said, smiling cruelly, "I don't think you would want to disobey me?" she said with an innocent smile.

"You aren't the type of person I would ever listen to! Who are you?!" The goblins cowered back. Maddie was unaware of this woman's true identity. Queen Lilith.

"Maddie, just listen to her," Brido whispered, panic embedded in his voice, "She's not who you think she is!" he said, staring at the queen.

"Who are you?" Maddie asked again, staring at the queen with a look of distaste.

"Why, the one and only Queen Lilith of course,"

she said with a cruel smile. Maddie's mean demeanor faded to fear. This woman has done so many evil things. But kidnapping a princess? That one was bad. Really bad. Maddie watched as the woman walked closer to Maddie.

"What do you need me here for?" Maddie asked, glaring.

"Ah, dear don't you look at me like that. I only want to see your skills. I won't tell you why, but you won't remember anything once you leave. If you leave alive."

"What do you mean by she won't remember?" Brido peeped with a small voice.

"None of you will remember anything! After I check out your skills to see if you are the chosen one, I will erase your memory and let you go. You must be wondering why," she said, clearly with no intention of explaining any further.

"Well, too bad! You may have magic, but you have no guards!" Maddie yelled.

"Oh, but I do…" Maddie's smile faded, "I see the invisibility spell worked," she said, cackling. With a flick of her hand, one-hundred or more guards dressed in black appeared.

"Whatever you want me to do, get on with it," Maddie said, fiddling with her fingers.

"Oh, nothing much, just a little obstacle course..." Maddie turned to see the queen flick her hand. Suddenly, a course appeared in the middle of the castle. Iron stakes sticking out of the floor, axes swinging from the walls, and a moat filled with a horrible smelling green liquid. There were a ton of other things which Maddie couldn't see very clearly, but she knew were going to be hard to deal with.

"You may begin, dear, and I allow your friends to watch!" she said, an evil grin visible.

Maddie took her first step and immediately, a clear barrier seemed to form between Maddie and the others. Maddie realized this when she ran towards the goblins, smacking into the barrier with a great amount of force. She had wondered why the goblins didn't run to her like she did them. However, she found out quickly they were put under a paralysis spell strong enough to keep them from moving at all.

Maddie walked over to the first obstacle: swinging axes. Axes were quickly swinging out from the walls, both the right and left. There was a moat underneath filled with a bubbly green acid. Maddie watched as a tiny little insect slipped into the acid, and slowly disintegrated to its death. The only part of the bug left was a tiny antenna sticking slightly above the pool of acid.

The acid seemed to be burping while a large amount of acid erupted onto the nearby ax swinging past it. Maddie felt her stomach tie to knots. *Oh god, what do I even do?* she thought, heart racing. The young girl figured impulse could only help her now. If she spent too much time strategizing, the ax will have been hit by acid too many times, causing it to slowly fall apart. Then, she would have no way across, and something told her Queen Lilith wouldn't be willing to help.

When the ax came swinging, she hopped on. A tiny part of her hand slipped and she found herself attempting to hold onto one of the sharpest parts of the ax. She slipped, cutting her hand and ended up dangling off the side of the ax that was swinging back and forward. She managed to move herself back onto the ax rope, but her hand was bleeding. *Nothing horrible*, she thought. *As long as I'm still able to move, this cut is the least of my worries.* Maddie swung from the rope that was holding it up. She hopped on to the next ax, clinging tightly and only trying to hold onto the rope and nothing more. She continued to do the same on the next three axes and made it across safely, minus the bleeding part of her hand. The queen watched, smiling her evil grin.

The next obstacle wasn't nearly as simple. Fire appeared to be shooting from the walls, and snakes filled the pit below. Cobra snakes. They hissed as Maddie approached closer. Every time Maddie moved, they uncoiled, ready to take a bite at Maddie's ankle.

Maddie saw 1 line of thick rope and figured out the best plan. It was going across the entire pit which meant it would help her get safely across. It was just high enough that if a snake attempted to bite, she wouldn't be touched. Maddie prayed that she would be able to muster enough strength to pull herself across. It was a one way trip.

The rope wouldn't support her weight again. If she turned back, there was no getting across. She would have to go quickly or it would surely snap halfway through. She grabbed the rope that was next to her and made sure it would be sturdy.

Maddie pushed herself to the rope and proceeded to put her hands in place. She was shaking uncontrollably. The cobras underneath her peered at her questioningly, as if they too didn't understand why she bothered to get so close. She began to move through, inching across the rope, dangling over the hissing cobras. She nervously went through the course, taken slow and steady breaths until she reached the end. As soon as she did, she collapsed to the floor out of nerves. Her legs were shaking, having almost been bitten by a cobra.

The last obstacle was made up from a bundle of sharp iron rods, rusted at the top, to not only ensure injury but also a bacterial infection for whoever stepped on them. They were sticking out all over the floor in every little corner and section of the course. But, they seemed to be withdrawing into the floor in sections, then popping back up but all at different times. She was to cross the floor, but Maddie seemed to be extra nervous on this one. She realized if she waited too long on a single spot of the room, she would be punctured by the iron rods.

The rods were sharp. Very sharp. Not only were they fast, but they had a gooey liquid on top of them.

Something told Maddie she should not ever try to touch it. Or else...bad things would most likely happen. Once she crossed that, she was to get onto the swinging axes once more to get to the other side. The swinging axes seemed to be the last course. Maddie longed to be in the peaceful zone away from the torture of this obstacle course. The front row of spikes went down first, so Maddie stepped onto the first row. Once the row began to come up, she ran to the next row, which now was empty of the iron rods.

Maddie repeated the process; however the last obstacle would be harder. She had to jump on the ax as soon as the needles rose from the floor. Otherwise, she wouldn't make it. The timing had to be very precise. If not, who knows what the fate of Maddie Shirkoff would be? Well, she did. And she had to make sure that would never happen. On the last needle filled row, as soon as they began coming up, she jumped, barely hopping onto the ax. Maddie stared at the cut on her hand. It was painful, yes, but not nearly as painful as it would have been to have gotten impaled by an ax.

As soon as Maddie finished the course, the obstacles all disappeared. Right back into the floors, walls, and ceilings. The queen walked up to Maddie, leaving the goblins all paralyzed. Maddie could see the anger in Samara's eyes, but she knew Samara could do nothing about it.

"One more thing, dear," the queen flicked her hand. Just then, a rusted metal ax swung at Maddie.

Maddie held her hands out to protect her face. It was a move straight from instinct, not rational thought. However, Maddie did not feel the ax hit. She looked up to see the ax, frozen by magic, a white light surrounding it. Maddie looked down at her own hands; also shrouded with the same white light. They were shaking. She felt strangely drained of energy, both physical and emotional, confused as well. The faint white light continued to emit itself from her hands, however Maddie neglected to give any serious thought to this.

Maddie looked at the queen and couldn't believe what had happened. Was it Maddie that froze the ax? Or did the queen do it just to see the reaction of the terrified young girl? Then again, she also tried to kill her. She just wanted to see Maddie terrified and afraid! The queen had no intention of murdering her but chose to do this for her own entertainment.

At least, that's what Maddie believed...she couldn't be one hundred percent sure after all.

"You are The One, dear...I CAN FEEL IT! Now, I shall erase your memory of this ever happening. You will find yourself wherever you were last. The goblins won't remember either...which is easy to believe since they have such small, pea-sized brains," she said, cackling and removing the paralysis spell off the goblins.

"Wait... why are you sending me back if I'm The One?"

Queen Lilith gave a laugh before answering, "I don't need you right now. The prophecy hasn't started yet. When it does, I'll know where to find you."

The goblins all stared at Maddie with a look of shock, but they never got to tell her what REALLY happened, because shortly after, they were whisked away back to the campsite. Almost like going back in time, but this was simply the queen's magic. So, Maddie prepared herself to wake up for the second time.

CHAPTER 11
THE BATTLE

At dawn, Maddie rose to see a face hovering over her. She could not remember anything about the castle, which was good, since traumatic experiences should be forgotten. It was Brido. His face was curved into a creepy grin as he shouted, "GOOD MORNING!"

"Ah! Can't you see that I was sleeping?!" she groggily murmured, unaware of the fact that she had TECHNICALLY already woken up.

"Chill out! I just came to drop this off," the goblin held out Sparky. The young girl lifted Sparky, placing his tiny body next to hers. Then, Brido continued, "and I came to let you know that breakfast is almost ready. Also, Ragon has bad news about this little...dying...dog," he finished at last. Maddie didn't want to know, but she rose, took a deep breath and went outside. Two voices were arguing. Samara and Ragon.

"I'm telling you! We need to give it to Sparky! Do you understand how devastated that girl will be if that dog dies in the middle of the journey?! Don't just use it for your selfish needs!" came the frustrated voice of Ragon.

"Well I'm sor-RY if I am angering you, but the last time I checked, you agreed with this plan entirely," Samara half shouted.

"Ummm…guys," Brido whispered as he pointed at Maddie, "she's coming…" both goblins stopped arguing and turned to see Maddie trudging through the grass who was unaware of the details of their conversation.

"What's the bad news?" she asked worriedly.

"Well, good morning to you, too," Samara responded with a grunt.

"Oh, I'm sorry. I am just so sick of constant Sparky issues," Maddie replied.

"T-t-that's…ok," Ragon said, stuttering and shaking as if he was about to be murdered. Which, although Maddie could not remember, she could definitely relate to., "anyway...umm, as you can s-s-see...Sparky is just getting w-w-worse. I-I-I don't know i-i-if you...ummm..." he began worriedly.

"Ragon," Maddie began, putting a hand on the goblin's shoulder, "you can tell me. No need to trip up on your words. I can take it," she said with a small smile.

"If you want to c-c-consider p-p-putting Sparky down to bear him the p-p-pain..." Maddie's mouth hung open in shock.

"Kill him?!" Maddie broke out, her eyes filled with tears. With this statement, not only had she felt betrayed, but also shocked. Not once had she ever thought that on this journey, Ragon, the animal lover, would ever think of hurting an animal, much less Sparky.

"It's just, you can't keep him in pain because you are too afraid to say goodbye," Ragon responded, his stuttering done now that he had gotten all his words out.

These words hit Maddie harder than ever. She understood that she couldn't be with Sparky forever, but she never thought that her last day with her little dog would be today.

"Please, just one more week. To search for a way to save him. He's my life. Please, you guys," Maddie begged through tears.

"Maddie," Ragon began, "Sparky is dying. He won't make it. He was trying to save you. Then, he got hurt. He is a hero. And sometimes, heroes lose their lives in the process of saving others."

"B-b-but Sparky...I love him," she sobbed.

"I know. But, people you love will eventually leave you. It isn't like Sparky will survive forever. He isn't immortal. He will either die today or tomorrow during the journey," Samara said in an attempt to be helpful. It really wasn't that helpful.

"And, you have had great memories with Sparky, right? Maybe...it's time to let him go?" Ragon asked quietly.

"I can't!" she sobbed, shaking. The goblins, seeing her desperate reaction, reluctantly agreed to allow Sparky to continue the journey.

Maddie focused on the task at hand, finding something to save Sparky and summoning the Great Doobi from his grave. As the journey continued, Maddie felt unusually nervous. The other land was dangerous, but she couldn't guarantee that this "walk-through" would be completely safe.

They trudged on by foot with no animals to carry them. The grass became so high that it touched just slightly above everyone's knees, which made it increasingly difficult to walk. The noises grew scarier the deeper into the forest they travelled. By the time the trudging part was over, the group had gotten themselves to a clear field that seemed to extend miles and miles in all directions.

"My word," Samara said through gritted teeth, "So many hours of walking and we go... NOWHERE!" she cried angrily.

"Well, I wouldn't say nowhere. Because now you can help me," said a faint, chilling voice. Maddie noticed Samara close her eyes in fear, as if remembering a tiny detail of some memory, but the memory wasn't there completely. Maddie turned around to see a dark-haired woman wearing a black dress filled with jewels.

The woman wore her hair up in a high ponytail. She wore a headband of diamonds and heels so dark, that at night, it would appear as if she was walking on air. "Allow me to introduce myself... unless, of course, we have already met" the air around them suddenly turned freezing cold. The ravens' call could be heard from a mile away. And the leaves of the trees slowly fell out, making rustling noises as they moved.

"Lilith," all three goblins said at once. Maddie's memories at once came flying back. The castle. The roses. The EVIL. THE OBSTACLE COURSE. No wonder she couldn't recognize her! Her memory had been erased! But Maddie didn't know if the goblins received their memories back. A faint smile shot from Lilith to Maddie, and Maddie figured the Queen had given her memories back purposefully. But why? Maddie remembered the goblins once more and looked at them, hoping they too had their memories. They clearly didn't, so it was no wonder they didn't look at her with the same awe on their face as they did before.

"Excuse me?" the queen asked, glaring at all the goblins.

"Queen Lilith," they all corrected. All Maddie could think was that this was the cruel, evil, frightening woman who had kidnapped Princess Kara.

"What do you want?" Maddie growled. She hoped she sounded braver than she felt.

"I want many things," the woman said as she picked up a leaf and crumpled it in her hand.

"Why are you bothering me? You-"

"Silence!" Maddie felt her mouth slam shut against her will. Her throat seemed to be closing up...

"LEAVE HER ALONE!" Samara bellowed. The queen simply laughed. And with a flick of her hand, Samara crumpled to the floor.

"This is much too fun," she said, clearly not caring about the pain she was causing. She let out a laugh. A cold laugh. The laugh alone made shivers run down Maddie's spine. Maddie took a step forward, rubbing her throat.

"Why are you here? First, you appear out of nowhere. Next, you knock out my friend. Why?!" Maddie asked angrily. The evil queen once again laughed her high pitched, cold laugh. The wind blew, making the queen's dress billow behind her. The evil queen raised her hand, bringing Samara back to consciousness. Samara immediately sat up and glared at the queen. Bad move. Samara's eyes opened wide as she put her hand to her throat, then to her head.

"Make the v-v-voices s-s-stop..." she muttered. Voices? What voices?

"Ahh. The voices. You want them to stop?" claimed the queen, "Of course...not. And if you don't like it...then there is even more of a reason to do it!" she cackled.

"What voices?" Brido said, stepping forward, "leave my sister alone."

"Bad times...I-I-I will n-n-never f-f-follow you...stop reminding me of bad times...I will NOT follow you. It will NEVER happen," Samara said, as she put her hand to her throat to stop herself from suffocating. The queen seemed to be enjoying this as she made sure the breaths became even shorter every second. After realizing what the queen was doing to her, she muttered, "I'm sorry."

"Ah. So brave. Such a brave goblin you are to demand something from me," she said, looking at Brido once again, "such a brave goblin. Such a dumb mistake," she twisted her hand in a gesture that could not have been good. Next thing Maddie knew, Brido was a beetle. And what did Lilith do next? She stepped on that beetle.

Brido was alive but was now writhing in pain. Ragon stepped forward and picked up the beetle.

"What you are doing is pure evil," Maddie yelled.

"You know what would be worse?" the queen did the same gesture and immediately, Brido was a goblin again. His arms were bent in ways they shouldn't have been, and his face was all cut up and bleeding.

"Brido..." Ragon whispered.

"This is a much better sight, don't you agree?"

"WHAT DO YOU WANT?! AND WHERE IS PRINCESS KARA?!" Maddie erupted, her hands clenched into fists. The faint glow emitted itself from her hands once more. Nearby, a tree came crashing down. Maddie neglected the incident and didn't give it a thought.

"And why do you want to know this?" the queen was about to switch the subject, but Maddie pressed on.

"Where is Princess Kara?" Maddie interrupted angrily.

"You dare interrupt me? Of all the-"

"Yeah, yeah. Now-"

"You are The One! I wouldn't kill you, just make you suffer. Unless I truly needed to...it would be such a waste of destiny. And for your princess...I will show you." The queen waved her hand and the princess appeared out of thin air. The princess looked the exact same as she did in the picture except that she was gagged and wore maid clothes. Her dark brown hair went down to her shoulder blades, and her tan skin reminded Maddie a lot of her own. Maddie sympathized with the princess who was held against her will and forced to work very hard. Maddie quickly changed her stream of thoughts and wondered what Queen Lilith meant by 'waste of destiny'.

"The One?" Maddie asked, still confused at what the queen had meant.

"Why, of course!" Queen Lilith responded.

"The One as in what? Another one of your slaves?" Maddie gestured to the princess that had been silently standing next to the queen.

"Of course not," the queen said, her pale face gazing upon Maddie. She grabbed Maddie's arm and continued, "imagine what we could do together, child." Maddie decided that she wasn't going down without a fight. The two remaining goblins removed the gag from the princess and ran to Maddie's aid. They were about to move Maddie away when the queen let go.

"Huh?" Maddie asked, confused.

"Oh, when will you ever learn, dear. I can't hurt The One."

"What do you mean…we could do things together? What could we accomplish?"

"The One…being The One is a privilege. It gives you power. But first, you must unlock your potential. I have given your memories back. Remember. What you did at the castle was something you have never done before."

"That doesn't mean I would ever want to work with you!" she cried angrily, "you clearly never think about anyone but yourself. I really don't know what The One is, but I don't intend on using the power for evil!"

While Maddie had been speaking to the queen, the goblins and Princess Kara were hiding behind a tree.

"We only have so much time!" Samara said, panicking, "we have to plan without Maddie!"

They all stared at the woman who seemed to be ready to rip them apart.

"What do we do?!" Samara whispered, looking back at the queen who was unaware of what the goblins were planning. Lilith was clearly angry with the goblins' disappearance but was more focused on grabbing Maddie. Maddie had run and hid somewhere in the grass while Lilith had been peering around for the goblins. The goblins hid behind the tree to continue their planning.

"Well, my parents always taught me that the palace has an emergency signal. Fire. Once the sparks from the first shoot up into the air, the army will come to your aid. They only told me and my sister. So, they will know it's me," Princess Kara stated.

"Wait," Ragon interrupted, "how come Lilith let you go so easily?"

Princess Kara took a breath, "I know. It's unbelievable. But, when she has a goal, she will get it. Whatever Maddie has or can do that Lilith wants, it's clearly something big. That's why she doesn't care about us. We aren't a big threat."

"Well, we have to at least try to save Maddie," Brido muttered.

"He's in horrible condition. How do we heal him?" Ragon asked the princess, gesturing to Brido.

"I would help but...this bracelet I am wearing," she started, "stops me from using my powers. It makes my magic too weak."

"Ragon, go grab a piece of wood and start a fire. Then, throw it into the sky...I know what to do," Samara ordered. Ragon ran to retrieve a spare piece of wood and start a fire. He grabbed the chunk of wood, lit it on fire and threw it into the air.

"Princess Kara, you have to answer quickly. The bracelet weakens your powers right...but they aren't gone completely?"

"That's right," she replied.

"I need you to make the fire fly higher and become brighter."

"I'll try," the princess waved her hand the burning piece of bark shone bright in the night sky...and you could see that many palace lights began to turn on from the distance. Even the calls of the royal army seemed to be getting louder. The plan had worked! However, the princess was left weaker. She had figured out how to use magic with the bracelet on. It clearly took up more energy than necessary.

Maddie watched from her hiding spot in the grass as the castle lights flipped on. The whole spot where the castle was seemed to be alive. If she squinted, she could see faint outlines of servants, in a frenzy, running around the castle.

"So...now you need help?" asked queen Lilith, "you can have it! Here is what I will do to you!" the queen moved her hand and a flash of light burst out. It was aimed at the tree the group was hiding behind. Just as the tree started to burn, Maddie had left her hiding spot in the grass to join the group.

"Dang it," Maddie said, staring at the burning tree. The second the flash hit the tree, toppling it to the ground. The tree, once alive, was now dead, shriveled by Two hits of fire. The group stared, terrified.

"DON'T YOU DARE!" cried the princess.

"I could quickly finish you...or I could hurt the goblin more..." she said, walking over to the goblins, Maddie, and Princess Kara.

"Try me," called the young princess.

"What are you doing?!" Samara hissed. This wasn't a part of the plan, "you'll get yourself killed! You don't have enough magic!"

The queen shot a bolt of light. The princess ducked, holding up the hand which held the bracelet that blocked her magic. The queen's bolt struck the bracelet, blowing it up and spraying bits and pieces of whatever was in it, everywhere. Immediately, the princess shouted over the queen's yells,

"WE NEED TO HOLD HER OFF UNTIL THE ROYAL ARMY COMES!"

"Wait! Princess! You need to heal Brido!"

"I'm-kind-of-doing-something-else-here!" she shouted over her own grunts. The princess may have been young, but she knew her magic. But, they all knew...she could only hold the evil queen off for so long. She shot a bright ray of blue, nailing the queen's ankle. The evil queen crumpled down in pain, giving the princess the ability to strike again. But right when the thin, bright red bolt was about to hit the evil queen, the queen, putting even more magic into it, reflected it, hitting the princess in the chest.

The young girl toppled over, hand on her chest. The evil queen smirked, "With that blast, you will never survive!" she said, glaring at the young girl.

"I will NOT die. Especially not at your hands," she said, glaring back at the queen.

"I can't promise that you will survive," the woman said, a smile etched upon her face.

"You can do it! Get up and try to keep fighting! Your family should be here soon!" Maddie yelled, trying to raise the princess's hopes.

"But, they aren't here right now. I could finish you if I wanted to... but I will wait. What is a better gift for your family than to see you die? You have been gone for ages. And now, they will find you, and they will try to free you from me. And, I will kill you right in front of them! They will adore the show!" she screamed.

"No. I have suffered because of you long enough," the princess began, "I will NOT let you treat me like this anymore. I will fight. I will fight to my last breath."

"Very well then. But I hope your will is ready!" she cried, the wind blowing, making her hair follow the wind's path.

"Will Brido be alright?" Maddie asked Ragon, gut wrenching inside her.

"They're only a few minor cuts. I'll be alright," Brido responded, managing a smile. "You should focus on the war that is ahead."

Maddie knew the cuts were horrible. Not to mention the dreadful sight of Brido's bones showing through the deep lacerations. His condition was better than Sparky's, but he was still in a dangerous state. Maddie hoped the royal army would hurry up. She didn't want to admit it, but...they were their last hope.

Maddie stared off into the distance, her gaze fixed upon the giant Royalis castle. The lights were on! There were horses shooting out from the castle! They were coming to the rescue! Maddie understood that the royals wouldn't be too thrilled to help Maddie, but she knew they would help as long as Kara was on their side.

Speaking of Kara, she thought. Maddie turned around. Kara had been shooting small spells at the queen while clutching her heart in pain. The spells had been becoming weaker every second. The family would have to get here fast if they still wanted a living child. After all, Kara did not look like she was on her way to victory. More like on her way to a hospital...

"The King has arrived! Leave the princess alone!" shouted one of the royal messengers who suddenly appeared out from a group of trees. An army of soldiers came in through a giant portal.

"Ah. My dear sister has arrived then?" Queen Lilith twisted her hand, leaving the messenger to fall to the ground, lifeless. The wind was blowing wildly now and the darkness set in, making the queen appear ten times more ominous. She knew the Royalis family would put up a fight to save their daughter.

The queen understood a big war was approaching. Staring at all the soldiers, it would be hard to think they were here for a tea party. The Royal Family's cavalry consisted of gorgeous white stallions. A knight in shining armor sat atop each one. Every knight carried a long, sharp sword. The weapons seemed to be constructed from solid gold while the entire hilt of the sword was solid diamond. These swords should have been incredibly heavy. But, the men who rode the horses were amazingly strong.

The evil queen managed to conjure up an army as well. But this army was ten times bigger than the Royal Family's. These men had muscles of steel, weapons meant to DESTROY, and armor that could deflect any weapon that crossed its path. They arrived on black horses, ready to slaughter the royal soldiers. They appeared out of nowhere, thirsty to fight an intense and bloody battle.

The Royal Family's knights had fear etched across each and every one of their faces. The evil army had armor that was colored solid black and its weapons were silver. While the Royalis army had weapons of gold and diamond, their armor was completely white. With the good and evil armies clashing, the war looked like a giant chess match played across the backdrop of a forest.

One of the king's soldiers, a good knight, tried to help Kara up, who had been lying on the ground. But an evil soldier stood in the way. The good knight, pulling out his sword, sliced the evil man in half, only to watch him multiply. The evil soldier had split into two. Once again, the knight stabbed the man. The evil knight multiplied into four, then, with each successive stab, he multiplied to eight, then sixteen, then thirty-two. The army seemed to be increasing with every hit, making them impossible to defeat.

The royal army was doing their best to hold them back, but the queen's army just continued multiplying after each physical brush. It was obvious that the royal army was going to lose if nobody came to their aid. Maddie was trying to punch and kick any and every evil soldier she saw. They didn't die only because they would multiply after any fatal hit, not when they were harmed with a minor injury... making every evil knight an undead warrior.

But there was one flaw that Maddie noticed amongst the fighting. The goblins stopped for a moment, as if they understood the same thing. Brido was safely hidden behind a tree. Kara was being protected by a knight who was now battling thirty-two soldiers. He would eventually lose, and Kara would be captured once again. The group had to think fast.

"Did any of you notice-" Maddie began.

"That Lilith was watching but also was making sure she wouldn't get distracted!" Ragon finished.

"She was watching the fight. But she stayed very careful. If anyone got within ten feet...they would be blasted apart! Because, they are possible distractions! If we can make the evil queen lose consciousness...WE CAN HAVE A CHANCE AT WINNING! The queen's consciousness keeps the soldiers alive. She needs to focus on the spell she is performing! But if she loses her level of consciousness, then her army will be defeated!" Maddie cried.

"That is completely correct!" Ragon said with a smile. "Then, when the war is over, we can heal Brido! But right now...we just have to focus on how to sneak up on her! We will need to use the back of a sword. It's nice and heavy and will most definitely

knock her unconscious! It will be a painful too!"
Ragon stopped smiling, "Oh no…" he muttered.

"What is it?" Maddie asked, worried.

"Princess Luna doesn't understand…she's calling
the dragons. She told me when I asked her what her
plan was! They will attack the army with fire, and
they will multiply faster than ever!" he said, in a serious tone.

Princess Luna whistled as loudly as possible. The
next thing Maddie knew, dragons swarmed left and
right, breathing fire at all the evil fighters. It was the
same clan Maddie had awkwardly run into during
the beginning of her journey in *Enchanted*! The
dragons looked just as they had before. Beautiful
with their fiery red scales and snake-like eyes. The
intensity of the war would only worsen with the
addition of fire. As the dragons swooped down into
the field, the clan took no mercy to the undead warriors. The fire blew in all places, hitting each and
every one of the evil fighters. Maddie could feel the
heat of the fire next to her face, and Samara unfor-
tunately was burned in the process of watching
("WHAT THE HECK?!" she shouted as fire singed
her cheek).

Some of the Royalis army began to run away because of the seismic multiplication of the guards. Others lost the battle because the undead made for fierce warriors. The few that had survived would end up meeting death very soon. Many of the good warriors had given up, and without their will to continue, all seemed hopeless. But the group was ready to put their plan into action. Samara ran to a good knight's corpse and grabbed the sword. Maddie got ready to sneak up on Queen Lilith but…someone grabbed her. Well, almost. It was what she felt before. A magic force squeezing her throat. The queen had suspected their plan all along! What could they do?

After a minute, her eyes rolled to the back of her head and her vision went dark. The war around her went foggy. "Maddie! Stay with me!" Ragon slapped her in an attempt to keep her awake. But, the evil queen did not like this, so, with a flick of her hand, Ragon was thrown back into a tree and knocked unconscious. Samara took the sword and hit the queen on the stomach instead of the queen's back. Not part of the plan? Sure. But effective…yes.

The queen, in pain, stopped the spell on Maddie. Queen Lilith swayed for a moment before losing consciousness. The evil army immediately fell to the ground. The soldiers were nothing more than puppets. They were corpses who had been raised from the grave to be used as pawns. The royal army looked around, confused. The dragons, who had been perched on the nearby mountain, swooped down to look around as well.

"How odd," said the large female Maddie had originally run into.

"Ooh! Mommy look! It's the runaway food we saw!" squeaked smallest dragon. The one who had peaked over the rock. Maddie glared at the baby dragon, annoyed with how inexperienced she had been at the time she had seen them.

"Take her away," the king said, bringing Maddie out of her memory. "Give her the magic blocking bracelet," he ordered the guards. Maddie watched as the guards approached the unconscious evil queen, flinching every time she took a breath. They placed the bracelet on her ankle, picked her up, and dragged her back to the castle to be locked up in the dungeon. Maddie rubbed her throbbing head.

"How do we thank you?" asked a voice behind them. It was the king, eyes filled with tears, holding his daughter, Princess Kara.

"Well…" Samara began. Maddie gave her a quick nudge.

"What Samara was going to say was…we don't need anything…" Maddie knew what they had done deserved a reward, but it was the least she could do after having ROBBED the Royal Family.

Samara looked at her and whispered, "There are things we need! A horse, food, water, a place to stay!"

Maddie glared at Samara, "We robbed them!" she cried as quietly as possible.

"YOU ROBBED THEM!" Samara said, giving Maddie a well-deserved slap in the arm.

"Fine," Maddie began. She looked the king directly in the eye and prepared herself. "There is something we could use during this hard journey," she began, staring at the king. Maddie trailed off but remembered what she had to say, "a horse. Well, two horses. To support us on our journey." The king thanked the group multiple times then called over a maid and had her bring two beautiful, white Stallions. "They-they're gorgeous!" Maddie said as she stared in awe at how beautiful these creatures were.

"And we are sorry-" Maddie began.

"YOU are sorry-" interrupted Samara.

"Yes. I am sorry about trying to take the magical ingredients...and the book..." she said meekly. "I just wanted to save my dog..."

"Normally, when a person steals something from our esteemed family, they get into a deep amount of trouble," said the queen, "But today, since you protected *Enchanted* AND saved my precious daughter, I can forgive you. All I ask is for my spell book back. You may keep the ingredients."

Maddie was relieved they didn't want their ingredients back since she had already used them. She also didn't want to see their reaction when they found out she possessed their missing key. So, she began to hurry things up...

"Thank you again...and now, we really have to go," she said as politely as possible.

"Don't mention it," the king began, "it's the least we could do after you saved our daughter." Maddie looked up to see the king, queen, and two princesses together at last-a TRUE Royal Family-

"Thank you," came a voice. It was Kara's, "all that time with her was torture. Day and night, I was to clean the castle. But not regular cleaning. I was to clean the deadly parts of the castle. When she wanted the basilisk cages cleaned, I was to do it. While the basilisks were still in there-"

Before the princess could finish, Maddie interrupted. "Wait, what's a basilisk?" she asked.

The princess smiled and began to speak, "You see Maddie, a basilisk is the king of snakes. It can kill you with a single glance. In our world, Lilith figured out how to breed these creatures. She is known as the mother of snakes. A woman who can make them listen to her." She continued her story. "then, when she was bored...she would beat me and torture me just to hear my screams of pain. She would use her magic to make me suffer in many ways. Once, she threw six deadly basilisks at me...because she knew I had no way to escape them. I was supposed to die today. But then, I appeared for no reason, gagged right in front of you. I never thought I would be rescued."

"Well," Maddie didn't know what to say, "I hope you are happy at last. And, thank you all for the horse."

The magnificent creature kicked its hoof at the ground. Her white color and dark brown eyes made her look like a goddess on four legs. What more could Maddie ask for? But then she decided what she needed.

"Do you mind healing Brido and Ragon?" she pleaded. The king nodded and lifted his hand. Instantly, Ragon returned to consciousness, and Brido's cuts healed, along with his body going back to normal.

Maddie wished they could do this with Sparky, but she knew only incredibly powerful magic could save him. After all, the poison that was injected into Sparky was not one the people of *Enchanted* were used to. Sure, Darkness Fangs were common, but it was common sense to steer clear of one. This was something Maddie had not known when she first stepped foot into *Enchanted*. The entire Royal Family wished the group luck on their journey. All three goblins, Maddie, and Sparky mounted onto the horse and set off into the distance, hopeful to finish their journey.

CHAPTER 12
MEDUSA

It had only been a couple hours after the battle, and Maddie held tightly onto the reigns of the horse. Ragon taught Maddie how to ride a horse and she had been having the time of her life. Occasionally, Ragon would correct her form, but other than that, she seemed to have a natural knack at riding horses.

"How much longer?" Maddie asked after switching positions with Ragon.

"It doesn't seem too far..." he turned quiet once more.

"Ragon...do you know where you're going?" Maddie asked hesitantly.

"Um..." a look of embarrassment crossed his face, "I heard a rumor that it was located not too distant from the royal palace. After the war, I figured it might be near the famous pond. The one where the Great Doobi fought his last battle."

"SO YOU DON'T ACTUALLY KNOW WHERE WE ARE GOING?!" Samara shouted.

"Samara!" Maddie cried, "don't yell at him! It actually makes sense...I like that idea, Ragon. Are we close?"

"Yes. We only have a little bit left to go," he said, relieved that someone supported his idea, "I figured this area because the people here are very sentimental. I believe they would have chosen his last victory spot as the place where he would be buried."

After about one hour more of riding, Samara pointed into the distance.

"Look!" she cried out in excitement. She waved her finger at a large castle

It looked like the type of castle that one would find in the Arabian desert. The palace pillars were made from white quartz. The iron doors stood perfectly in view. Something about this beautiful building drew Maddie towards it. The castle had a powerful glow. As if many things had happened there that only a true hero could understand. The aura of power felt so strong that Maddie thought this could be the place that would heal Sparky once and for all.

"It's the palace of the Great Doobi. You know, the brave, mighty, and powerful dog that protected *Enchanted*," Brido said in awe, "we can finally get what we want!"

"But, what about Sparky?!" Maddie shouted. She took a good look at her brown bundle of joy. His wounds were completely open as blood and bits of poison leaked out. The poison had affected him to the point where he now had lost weight and looked very shriveled.

"Don't worry, there ought to be some sort of powerful magic in here. I mean, just look at the size of this place!" Brido interrupted excitedly. The group walked in and looked at an immaculate palace. It was as if it were cleaned on the hour every hour. But, by whom? Maddie silently walked through the entryway, footsteps echoing with every step.

"Who goes there?" asked a cold, cruel, and deep female voice. Maddie peered around the corner to see a woman with green scales for skin, snakes for hair and armor of solid bronze. The bronze was so dirty that this terrifying woman couldn't even see her own reflection in the armor.

"Medusa. She can turn you into stone if you look into her cold eyes. You don't want to get caught being here with her. I hear she isn't very kind to her visitors," Ragon shakily whispered. He hugged Sparky closer to his chest, "this dog won't last through another monster battle," he stated.

Medusa's feet seemed to move so gracefully. It was as if she was walking on air. Maddie turned to watch the serpent-like woman glide through the halls as if she owned them. No! These halls belonged to Doobi. So, what drew her here?

"Why is Medusa in this world?! Medusa is from Greek mythology!" Maddie said in shock.

"There you go again," Samara muttered, "haven't you learned anything? Your world says it is mythology. They are all real here. These things aren't just what you read about in books. They are actually alive. They are real, not myths, so would you stop getting all shocked about it?"

"Medusa is a serpent woman. She is cruel and mean. There is no telling what she will do to you if she captures you for any reason and decides NOT to turn you to stone," Brido whispered.

"But she is in GREEK mythology! Not fairy tales! I refuse to believe she exists!" Maddie said, eyes screaming in protest.

"Look, a lot of things you wouldn't possibly believe are here. And they are dangerous," Samara responded.

"I sniff...company!" Medusa cackled. Maddie and the goblins took a step back. Samara looked as if she was about to sneeze.

"No. Not now Samara," Maddie pleaded.

"Ah...ah...ah...chooooooooo!" Samara sneezed abruptly and proceeded to trip over her feet. She fell backwards and she knocked herself into a table, a vase flying off. Medusa started walking over in the direction where the group was hidden. "Sorry," Samara whispered, "but, I don't really know how to defeat this woman."

"Come, come children," she cackled, "tell me where you are! I just want to introduce you to my-self!" she let out a laugh, more like nails dragged against a chalkboard. It was so high pitched, so unreal.

"You guys, we have to kill her by dropping something on top of her. I don't know how she got in here, but she won't stay long!" Maddie cried.

"Lilith won't stop me. She may have been bad to you, but I will torture you more!" Medusa said, slithering towards Maddie, unaware of her plan.

Maddie looked over at the tall statue and thought if she could knock it over and somehow hit Medusa, she could defeat her and stay safe. Maddie kicked over the second vase, and when Medusa came over to turn them to stone, the statue toppled over and fell on top of the dreaded woman-creature.

"You think she's dead?" Ragon asked, hugging a terrified Sparky.

"No," Medusa laughed. She immediately rose from the ground, completely unscathed, "I can't see that happening anytime soon. BUT YOU WILL BE!" Maddie turned to see Brido's horrified look.

"I refuse to die today!" Brido cried out. Medusa grabbed Samara and pulled the goblin close to her face, staring deep into her eyes. In only one second, Samara had already been turned to cold, hard stone.

"No!" and for the first time ever, Maddie saw Brido cry.

"Aw. Brido, I know you loved Samara. I will miss her very much. But, we have to keep moving!" Maddie whispered to them, "unless you want the same thing happening to us…"

Medusa glided over. "Why are you chasing us?!" Maddie asked under her breath as they continued to run from the evil mythical character that was supposed to have never existed. The loss of Samara had hit everyone hard. Ragon was holding Sparky quietly. Maddie was too shocked to speak. Brido was bawling his eyes out.

"Lilith told me you could be The One. She had come over to gloat and say she found you. Being The One…you could bring me to power and break my dreaded curse. You would be the protector of the realms! The power!" she cried, "when I summoned the original great sorcerer, he would not permit me to have any power. For I already had too much. He said, in order to gain, I had to give up all my power. I had to start with nothing. I had traveled incredibly far. When I found the spell book of the gods, the Greek ones, mind you, I searched through it, desperate to find the spell that would lead me to gain all the power possible. I was too powerful for my own good. You, perhaps being The One, can assist me. You could break that rule. We can work together!" Medusa cackled.

There it was again. The One. What could this possibly mean?

"Us?!" Maddie yelled in shock.

"Yes. You can have all you desire if you let me do one last thing," Medusa answered.

"Ok, and what would that be?" Maddie knew she would never agree but was curious to see where this question might lead.

"Let me dispose of your pesky so-called 'friends'. Just let me turn them to stone so we can begin working together." The two remaining goblins each turned around in shock, afraid of what Maddie's response might be. But Maddie had a basic plan. She would rip the mirror off the wall and shove it in Medusa's face. Medusa would see her own reflection and should turn to stone. Apparently, if you said no to Medusa, or even tried to hurt her, the only option was to live the rest of your life as a statue. Would Maddie even be able to use Medusa's own powers against her? That was the plan.

"I'll never work with you!" she cried. Avoiding any eye contact, Maddie dashed down the hall, pulled a mirror from the wall, and as Medusa shifted to look at Maddie in the eye to turn her to stone,

Maddie inserted the mirror in front of her face. Medusa was now officially face-to-face with her own reflection.

"No!" Medusa cried. And as fast as Samara had turned to stone, Medusa turned to stone as well.

"We're sorry for ever doubting you, Ragon said quietly. Maddie flipped around to see the remaining two goblins crying over Samara's body. Maddie walked over to Samara. She stood over the goblin, crying. Without noticing, she dropped a tear on Samara's head. In a split second, Samara began to glow. Samara's stony body had once again turned to flesh.

"How...how...what?" Brido asked, releasing a shaky breath.

"What do you mean?" Maddie asked, wondering why he looked so shocked.

"Your tear...never mind. I'm sure I'm just seeing things. Or...yes. It was just a coincidence," said Brido, sighing. Each goblin and Maddie gave a group hug.

"After this, I think we can deal with anything!" Maddie stated, breathing a sigh of happiness and relief.

Suddenly, the palace doors opened wide, and a voice spoke out, "It's such a mess in here! What could have happened-," the mysterious figure turned to face the group, "so it was you. And you have arrived."

Although Maddie did not know, this person would be the most powerful being they had yet encountered. What would happen next was unknown.

Chapter 13
The Enchantress

Maddie turned to face a tall woman with long, wavy, blonde hair wearing an extended white dress with a flowing cape. Maddie was reminded of the attire, which mythical goddesses were said to wear. *But that was supposed to happen only in books,* Maddie thought with a sigh. The lady's skin was light, almost pale. Her beautiful appearance simply impressed Maddie.

Her dress was drawn out, and it trailed the floor. The sleeves of the dress were lengthy as well, leaving a giant but stylish opening at the hand. Unlike superheroes, this cape seemed to flow like the wind, making the strange lady look unusually stunning. Her icy blue eyes seemed to pierce Maddie's soul, searching for every trace of good.

Her makeup was applied perfectly. She wore sparkly white eyeshadow and light pink lipstick. Her eyeliner was applied flawlessly in the cat-eye style, and her mascara made her lashes appear curly and long. Despite her kind face, the group was terrified. She waved one hand and the room was instantly spotless from the mess Medusa had made during the time she occupied the castle. Even Medusa's body had now disappeared with the wave of this magician's hand.

"That's better," she said approvingly. Maddie watched the woman walk up to them, unsure of what to do or say.

"Look ma'am, we mean no harm. If you are another crazy person getting ready to fight us...then." Maddie looked at the goblins, "We're ready."

The mysterious woman smiled and responded in a soft laugh, "No. I would never think of hurting another person, let alone an animal," she added, gesturing to the whimpering puppy.

"Who are you? And, please forgive my quick introduction. We have been attacked a lot lately, so I expected the worst. I am Maddie. I'm from Arizona. These are my companions. Samara, Ragon, and

Brido. Over there, in Ragon's arms is Sparky, my dog," Maddie said to the woman standing in front of her.

The lady smiled once more and answered Maddie's question, reading her mind flawlessly, "I am the enchantress of *Enchanted*. My name is Rose, but I am referred to as the enchantress. I would be more than happy to have the honor of helping the traveler from afar," Maddie smiled at her. Not only was she smart, but she had the best feature that Maddie could ask for. Kindness.

"Well, I do understand that you aren't SUP-POSED to be a threat, but how am I supposed to believe you? You walk in here, with MAGIC. The last encounter we had with a magical human being resulted in a dungeon, a knocked-out person, and a burnt croissant," Maddie said, eying the enchantress with a solid amount of suspicion.

The enchantress once again laughed her soft, warm laugh, looking quizzically at Maddie, waiting for an explanation on the croissant part of her story. That never came. Instead, the enchantress looked up and began to speak, "I understand, the journey here might not have been easy...but I am well known throughout *Enchanted*. I am acquainted with many things such as why you are here and all the things you wish to discover. But, if you are to survive during your short period of time here, you need to trust me. Like I said, I am well known here. Just ask your little friends."

Maddie looked at Samara, Brido, and Ragon, waiting for a response. To her surprise, they all nodded their heads. If her friends truly trusted this woman, then so would she.

"Dear, I know why and how you are here. The important part is...you have reached this palace alive. I DON'T need another dead hero incident..." she muttered. Maddie stood, gaping at the lady in front of her. Dead hero?! What type of a comforting statement was that?! Maddie looked at the now clean building that was restored to its former glory. The giant pillars made of quartz, and the floor that was made of white marble. It was a beautiful sight. The only issue that concerned Maddie was the rooms, however.

There were multiple rooms. Not just Doobi's, she guessed. They were all probably very important, but the only room she would come to care about would be The One that could save her dog.

Maddie wondered what "The One" could be about and how the enchantress knew Maddie was here, but her mind was on other things. She would finally be able to save Sparky if she could just wander throughout this place for a bit. *No. This woman is ten times more powerful than the Royal Family. It would be downright stupid to wander around here*, she thought scolding herself. After a while, the enchantress led them to a door. "In this room, you will see the spirit of the Great Doobi." The goblins' bodies trembled with excitement. Maddie, however, could not have been more enraged.

"What about Sparky?!" she yelled.

"The Great Doobi will examine Sparky and determine how to help him," the enchantress answered. Maddie didn't want to go in the room without having asked a few more questions.

"You are an enchantress?" she asked hesitantly.

"Yes," the enchantress responded.

"And you are going to show us Doobi?"

"Yes," the beautiful woman said, patient with Maddie's redundant questions. Her grace towards Maddie was shocking.

"Could I be a powerful magician like you since I am the 'chosen one'? That seems ridiculous. And you have been the one cleaning up this castle?" Maddie demanded.

The enchantress paused before answering these questions, "The first one is simply a myth. It could be possible. I have no proof you are the chosen one...but, your personality says otherwise. I would need to get to know you better to determine this. But, there is one thing blocking me from believing you are the chosen one...you don't have magic. Also, the reason I am so skeptical is because Medusa wanted to gain power so badly that she was willing to believe anything. And yes, out of respect for Doobi, I clean this palace. I will explain more about the chosen one with Doobi."

"Can we go in now?" Samara asked impatiently. The enchantress nodded.

"There is a special key needed for all to go in. My magic can only allow me, and only me, inside," she sighed.

"You mean this key?" the goblins turned in shock as Maddie held up the key to the enchantress. The one she had magically glued to the key around her neck.

"How did you come to receive that?" the enchantress asked quietly.

"What do you mean?" Maddie asked, wondering. The goblins all stood, staring at her, eyes open and mouth wide. Whatever Maddie held was not something that was common. However, it had been for her. The original key belonged to her grandfather, and it was later gifted to her in a necklace. The other had been stolen from the Royal Family.

"I am the only one who can reach and open Doobi's door...that key opens all doors of Enchanted. You would need the king and queen's special key to do it! In addition to the sacred advisor key of the great Alecondrus! How...unless...you are a descendant! But I can sense you had to steal one of the keys. Let me guess, the royal one?" she finished.

"Um, yes?" Maddie said, voice shaking, "I'll return the key! I promise!"

"They can always make a key to open every door in the castle. It is just what this one was made out of. The founding stones of *Enchanted*. I will let them know you have it, but once they find out you could be The One, they would probably be happy to let you keep it!"

"Probably?" Maddie asked, immediately nervous.

"Definitely!" the enchantress responded, "but do tell me your story."

Once Maddie explained the story to clarify what the enchantress wanted to know, the lady calmly stuck the key into the door and pushed it open. They were only a moment away from entering the room of the Great Doobi.

CHAPTER 14
THE GREAT DOOBI

The room had marble flooring and walls with four pillars standing at the entrance. In the middle of the room was a fountain with a cement gravestone standing upright. The stone read:

The Great Doobi

R.I.P

July 13-December 8

A wise and loving dog that was a skilled warrior
who fought for the sake of Enchanted.
May this loving dog rest in peace

Maddie's followed as the others bowed their heads to pay respect and remember the amazing dog. As Maddie watched this sad scene, she felt a little bad for trying to hurry things up in order to save Sparky. The goblins had focused on Sparky the entire journey; it was now their turn to have what they had asked for.

Maddie watched Brido remove a jar filled with a clear liquid and pink rose petals at the bottom from his bag. At first, she was confused. Then, she realized that it was the item taken from the trapdoor at the Royal palace. "That is the magic used to summon Doobi. Would you like to use it? It is quite powerful," the enchantress asked.

"Wait," the goblins stopped dead in their tracks. "what else can this potion do?" Maddie asked hesitantly.

"The petals used to put Doobi back to rest are also used as a healing potion," the enchantress replied. Maddie slowly turned to look at the goblins while the enchantress continued to speak, "I don't understand why you decided not to use it on Sparky. Clearly Maddie wants him to be safe."

"Yes," Maddie growled, "why didn't you use it on Sparky?!" she asked, breathing heavily. Maddie grabbed Sparky from Ragon.

"I was trying to convince them-" Ragon began.

"Obviously, you did a poor job! And why should I believe you anyway?! If you truly wanted Sparky alive, you would have secretly told me, no matter the cost!" she shouted.

"Yeah well, we didn't even know you," Samara began, "and it's not our fault that you were stupid enough to go into the portal in the first place!"

Maddie was a little shocked that Samara knew about the portal and was even more shocked that she would say such a thing.

"And you came to bother us in the first place. You should've done this journey yourself!" Brido cried.

"It is rightfully mine! It was with my key you opened the trapdoor!"

"Stop," the enchantress said, glaring at everyone, "look at yourselves. Arguing like little fairies." Maddie didn't quite understand the comparison, but everyone else seemed to understand and turned quiet.

"We-" Brido attempted to speak, but the enchantress abruptly shushed him.

After a pause, Ragon opened his mouth, "I really did try to get them to use it on Sparky."

"It's true," Samara managed, quietly.

"The potion," Ragon continued, "has liquid to wake up Doobi and petals to put his spirit back into the grave. The petals are also used for healing." Maddie looked longingly at the petals.

"Go ahead," Maddie sobbed, "I can let him go." It was obvious that she couldn't, for someone that important to you cannot just be taken away.

"This is wrong. I don't know if we should do this," Ragon said quietly.

"Are you kidding?!" Samara responded. This is our chance to see Doobi! Why would you give that up?"

"Because Samara, it isn't ours to use. Maddie is right…it's hers."

"No. She gave it to us fair and square."

"She really didn't," Ragon replied, fuming.

"Whatever," Samara responded angrily. She proceeded to pour the potion onto the grave. Ragon and Brido each let out a gasp.

"Samara!" Ragon cried.

There was a swirl of fog and in a split second, Doobi's figure appeared. He was a white colored Golden Doodle with a light sky blue collar. His hair was curly and clean. All of the goblins trembled with excitement.

"Well, hello there," came his sweet voice.

"Why, we are just so excited to meet you!" Ragon cried. Each goblin bowed down to Doobi.

"You have summoned me. Is there anything you need help with," he offered, "I can always lend a hand for a fellow *Enchantedian*."

"We are in need of a way to gain power and money. You see, Mr. Doobi, it is quite hard to live in our conditions. We rescued Princess Kara from the evil queen, Lilith, and were offered a reward. In an attempt to be humble, we declined. We only took supplies we needed for our journey. Sadly, my siblings and I are in need of a place to live and want to find a way to obtain this. Although we love our cave, we are shut away from modern life. We wish to live amongst other goblins. Even if we can't, a home would be nice. We only have the bare minimum of food and water in our cave," Samara finished.

"Well, you need to approach the king and say that I told you to request a home built for you. Tell him, that earlier, you did not think of this need when he had asked the question. That should solve your issue. I give you this letter with my approval," Doobi answered wisely. A letter formed from thin air. It slowly drifted towards the goblins until it was eagerly snatched up by Samara.

"Thank you, sir!" all three goblins said at once.

"Now, let me send it to them through magic," the enchantress began, "it will be much easier," she flicked her hand, and the letter disappeared.

"Are there any more questions?" Doobi asked.

"Yes," Maddie began, "these goblins used a potion that they found in the trapdoor of the Royal castle to summon you. That trapdoor was opened with my grandfather's key. First, I don't understand whether my grandfather has been here or not. Second, why did the portal appear in the first place. Third, how will I save my dying dog? Those petals that are also meant to put your spirit back into the grave are meant to also save my dog. Please tell me there is a way to save him," she began to cry.

"Well, my dear. Your grandfather, Alecondrus, used to live here. He was born in the city of Hazakia. At the time, there was a different generation of the Royal Family. The Royal Family that you know now happened to be children at the time. I shall tell you the story. It will help you understand more. Lilith had grown up as the youngest child. Thus, she was second in line to the throne. She knew she would never truly gain it, for there was no way the future king and queen would pass in time for her to rule for a lengthy period. While she was a princess, she wanted to be known as a powerful force when it came to helping the Royal Family. When she tried to kill the king, her own father, and the other princess, her sister, a bracelet was made by your grandfather that could block her magic. He defeated Lilith when *Enchanted* needed him most. Thus, in his honor, a city was named after him. Alecondrus. After that, he received constant praise. Your grandfather had been able to lock up Lilith for many years. He was awarded a position of Royal Advisor. He had always heard of the myths of your world. A world of no magic or problems. Time does not pass here nearly as fast as it does in your world. He appealed to me for advice, and I had Rose, the enchantress, conjure up a portal to your world. He stepped through, taking his advisor key with him. However, you may be wondering why. He felt that, at the time, every moment a problem occurred, he would be called. He didn't want to have the burden of being a hero when, to himself, he was just a normal man. By taking the advisor key, he made sure no other man would be forced into this position of constant fear of not being enough. He truly felt overwhelmed and carried the burden with him. He wanted to know where he could go to escape the troubles of the magic world."

"Wow. He really never seemed that cool...what are the other cities called?"

"The capital is Doobi. It is followed by Ale-condrus. Then you have Laksont that neighbors Alahara. Alahara is a city to the north of Misawa. Then you have the major trading city, Maripont."

"They all sound like weird names."

"They are. Names...not necessarily weird here. Alahara and Misawa are *Enchanted's* military gener-als. They control how *Enchanted* fights. They had cities named after them because they worked to-gether to plot an attack that would defend *Enchanted* when the evil giant Gor attempted to destroy our land. He is a giant Darkness Fang with no mercy. He is also very dangerous and smart. Many people had died attempting to fight him. But, we had the greatest military generals of all. Very impressive, what they did. When you arrived, you defeated Gor's child, Osam. He was pretty big and stupid.

Normally, we find darkness fangs incredibly dangerous. However, this specific one did not live up to his father's name. The royal army was planning to get rid of him, but you seemed to take care of that problem. The last city is Maripont named after a famous chef that had started off poor but became very rich from performing the activities she loved. So many people looked up to the way she transitioned her lifestyle from powerless to powerful. It was such a large spectacle that the public convinced the Royal Family to name a city after her."

"Wow. That's amazing. Now, can you answer my other two questions? Please, I'm just so anxious to hear what you have to say!"

"Of course. Why did the portal appear? The portal will only appear when summoned. I will let Rose cover this for you since she is the reason you are here." Doobi said, his shimmering body now facing Rose the Enchantress.

The Enchantress let out a sigh and began to explain, "I heard a mortal with a special ability would come to this land to solve a problem. I can't tell you what the problem is because I don't know if you are The One. I had been watching you carefully, checking to see any extra good features. You seemed to be normal. You were brave and athletic. You crossed through this land even in the hardest conditions. You were chased and fought a battle against QUEEN LIILITH. That right there deserves praise. You were kind to those who surrounded you and wouldn't let anyone cruel cross your path. This is a quality that will serve you well in our world. Though you didn't seem to have any special abilities, you did seem to act brave and strong. Even before you coming here, I had sensed you would be a good candidate for this land. I wanted to see how you behaved in our world, so I summoned the portal. It was a risk, doing it so close to other houses, but you walked right in. I shut the portal as soon as you entered. That's why it disappeared. However, though it doesn't seem you have magic, I believe you don't really know what you are truly capable of."

"You knew where I lived?!"

"I had to track you down. It wasn't to harm you. Just to check if you were The One. Which, with further exploration, you could be. You are the first in many years to have almost all the qualities The One should have. And about me knowing where you live…it's better than Lilith knowing," the enchant-ress huffed.

"Oh," Maddie shivered at the thought.

Doobi began to speak once more, "For the third question. How to save your dying dog? Darkness fang poison can be incredibly deadly. Sadly, the rose petals are the only way," Maddie's face fell, "but I have been here for many years answering questions for travelers. The only way to get into this room however, is with your key. The keys only merged because of one trait. Each key you used to assemble this dog key, was made from the found-ing stones of *Enchanted*. As soon as your grandfa-ther left with the other key, nobody had been able to visit this palace. People would arrive, only to realize they could not enter. And, I love the people that look up to me, but I feel that it is time that I have eternal peace. You may use the petals on Sparky. The enchantress can finally put me to rest with her magic."

Maddie stood there, shocked at the kind deed this dog was willing to perform, "Thank you," she whispered with tears in her eyes. "You don't un-derstand how much this means to me," Maddie approached Doobi, giving him a hug, "your family loves you so much," she added.

Maddie grabbed a handful of petals and sprinkled them on top of Sparky. Slowly, Sparky's cuts began to close. His broken bones began to mend. After about a minute, Sparky was a healthy dog again. Whimpers could no longer be heard. Maddie cried out in happiness as Sparky sweetly licked her face. "I'm ready," came Doobi's voice, "tell my father, Caimal, my mother, Rosa, and my sisters, Kara and Luna, that I love them all. That I wish I could've been able to be alive with them one more day," the enchantress waved her hand over Doobi's spirit. Maddie looked at Doobi. He looked happy and healthy. His smile was the best thing a girl could ask for.

"Rest well, baby boy," came four voices. It was the Royal Family. After being notified by the enchantress that Doobi had been summoned, they had magically left the castle and appeared in Doobi's hallway. They entered easily since the door had been left open. Maddie didn't even hear them enter. "We'd give anything to spend one more day with you as well. We love you too." The Royal Family all gave Doobi one big hug. After the hug, Doobi disappeared. Not one person in the room didn't have watery eyes.

After everyone had calmed their emotions, the king spoke, "We have your house ready. A big mansion by the Enchanted beach. And Maddie, you may keep the key, for I do feel that you are the chosen one."

"Thank you so much!" all three goblins practically yelled at the same time.

"Th-thank you!" Maddie said, obviously very behind with the timing. "Ma'am," Maddie asked the enchantress, "do you think you can send me home now?"

"Of course. But wait," the Enchantress said as Maddie turned around, "take this," the lady handed Maddie a necklace with a shell on it. A white conch shell. These were the same type of shells that Maddie used to listen to the waves with her mother in California.

"What's this for?" Maddie asked.

"This will allow you communicate with the goblins. You need to voice the name of the goblin you want to speak to. Or you can say that you want to talk to them all. You must say this into the shell, and it will allow you to speak directly to them. In order to pick up, just hold the shell to your ear. It will create a vibration on your chest to let you know if someone is calling you. You will always know when to pick up. Be careful. If it breaks or is even gets scratched one bit, the magic will drain from it and it will become a normal shell." The enchantress added this last point as she gave one shell necklace to each of the goblins.

"Well, thank you so much. But, how are you planning to send me home?" Maddie followed up.

"I will summon the portal. I am also planning to keep an eye on you. You have potential to be the chosen one," The enchantress said, smiling. Maddie watched as the enchantress waved her hand, and the swirling ball of light was in front of Maddie once again. Maddie handed the enchantress the dog key and smiled. She knew she had the opportunity to keep it...but, it just didn't feel right. *Enchanted* was a place that she would never really come back to. It felt better to leave it with the people who loved and cared for the land more than she ever could. The portal's winds blew Maddie's hair as she stared into it. She hadn't seen this ball of light in what felt like months. It baffled Maddie to know it had been at least two weeks she had spent in this crazy world. She recalled the day she was transported. It had been a different time, and she had been a different person. Maddie looked at the goblins and gave them each hugs.

"Thank you for making this trip entertaining. And I forgive you." Maddie smiled the biggest grin the goblins had seen since they met her.

"Well, goodbye then," Samara whispered in Maddie's ear.

"Don't forget to keep in touch," Brido reminded her, gesturing to the necklace around each of their necks.

"We'll miss you," a voice from behind Maddie whispered. It was Ragon.

"I'll miss you all! I promise to keep in touch! And Doobi," Maddie said as she began to tear up, "if you can hear me... thank you. Words can't describe how much I appreciate what you did."

Maddie looked at them for one second, then leaped into the portal with Sparky. And in a flash, they were gone.

Chapter 15
Coming Back!

Maddie felt the familiar sensation of heat. She smiled to herself. She was back in Arizona. She thought of the faces of the goblins who had been so kind to her. Her heart ached with a longing to give them all one more goodbye hug. She looked at Sparky, who was happily wagging his tail and running around in the dirt. She thought of Doobi's generous offer and hoped he was happy. Maybe he is at the rainbow bridge where dogs are supposed to cross once they pass from this world?

She thought of the battle against Lilith and Medusa...and for a split second, she never wanted to step foot in that land ever again. But after the second passed, the longing to return appeared. She wanted to be near the goblins and thank the enchantress. She had spent weeks in that world, so she couldn't help but miss it. She immediately remembered her mother, father, and sister. Darting toward her house, panic filled her mind. How long had her mother been searching for her? Would her parents be mad or relieved? Were they worried?

She ran in through the front door with Sparky trotting by her side, "Mom! I missed you so much! You must have been so wor-"

"Dear lord, Maddie," her mother cried, accepting the hug from her daughter, "I was just calling you to get you out of your room for figure skating! What has gotten into you? You pretend like you have been gone for two weeks and then sneak up on me like that! Maybe you are doing too much ice-skating," her mother replied, laughing. Maddie's mother's smile seemed to light up the room.

"You mean, no time has passed at all?" Maddie's smile turned to a frown. Was time in this world much slower? Well, she shouldn't have been surprised. That's what Doobi had said, after all. She just didn't know it was THAT slow.

"Maddie, you just saw me thirty minutes ago. Why would you even think like this? And, what are you wearing? You get changed then head out the door for practice. We are going to be so late. Thirty minutes and you haven't gotten dressed!" she sighed, "I'll drive you there. Daddy is coming home from work and Avery has just gone to her friend's house. She left fifteen minutes ago. Remember? Anyway, go get dressed. And when you get into the car, get ready for the longest lecture you've ever had!" Maddie's mother laughed, then gave Maddie a kiss. *Yep*, Maddie thought, *home sweet home.*

Epilogue
One Year Later

Maddie turned twelve and had worn the necklace every day. She liked to talk to the goblins before bed just to hear how things were going in *Enchanted.* Apparently, the Royal Family had made a new city in honor of the goblins and Maddie. Maddie wished she could be back there with them in *Enchanted. Maybe, just maybe...*she liked to think, *a problem would arise, and they would call her back.*

She knew that it was a bad thing to think about, but she couldn't help it. She desperately wanted another adventure that was as magnificent as The One that she had faced the year before.

As she tucked herself into bed, she couldn't help but think...

ABOUT THE AUTHOR

Danit Knishinsky is a thirteen-year-old girl who was born in New Jersey and spent most of her life in Arizona. She has been ice-skating since she was five years old and has always wanted to be an actress. She runs the YouTube channel, "Danit K", and has been writing stories her entire life. The story you just read was inspired by a tale which Danit wrote when she was only eight years old. Her writing has improved since this book, and she is working on many more novels.

If you enjoyed this book, make sure to follow Danit on her website, DanitBooks.com, her Instagram, and YouTube channel so you can be notified whenever her latest books are released!

WEBSITE: DanitBooks.com

INSTAGRAM: DanitK_Official

YOUTUBE:

Tips and Tricks (books and stories-so you can become an author as well!): Danit K

Made in the USA
Middletown, DE
06 June 2021